"I want th...
of my chi...

Karen's ston...
at Hal's sugg...
want," she s... ...ell, I'm
not Kirsty."

He appeared completely
unperturbed. "I'm well aware of that.
Kirsty died in my arms, remember? It's
you I want."

"It's an impossible situation," Karen
whispered.

"Not at all," he denied. "It's quite clear-
cut."

She stared at him, looking desperately
for a chink in his armor. "I've always
hated you," she said.

"Your last marriage was presumably
based on love, but it didn't work.
Perhaps hate is a better basis for
starting with. After all, things can't get
worse. They can only improve."

EMMA DARCY nearly became an actress until her fiancé declared he preferred to attend the theater *with* her. She bacame a wife and mother. Later she took up oil painting—unsuccessfully, she remarks. Then, she tried architecture, designing the family home in New South Wales. Next came romance writing—"the hardest and most challenging of all the activities," she confesses.

Books by Emma Darcy

HARLEQUIN PRESENTS

648—TWISTING SHADOWS
680—TANGLE OF TORMENT
823—DON'T PLAY GAMES
840—FANTASY
864—SONG OF A WREN
882—POINT OF IMPACT
903—MAN IN THE PARK
921—A WORLD APART
935—THE IMPOSSIBLE WOMAN
960—WOMAN OF HONOUR
984—DON'T ASK ME NOW
999—THE UNPREDICTABLE MAN

EMMA DARCY

the wrong mirror

Harlequin Books

TORONTO • NEW YORK • LONDON
AMSTERDAM • PARIS • SYDNEY • HAMBURG
STOCKHOLM • ATHENS • TOKYO • MILAN

Harlequin Presents first edition October 1987
ISBN 0-373-11020-0

Original hardcover edition published in 1986
by Mills & Boon Limited

CHAPTER ONE

KIRSTY was dying.

Karen knew it even as she struggled into consciousness. Shock jerked her upright in bed. It was not a nightmare. She didn't know how she could be so sure, yet she was. It was a truth as implacable as . . . as a law of the universe. Inescapable.

And, just as relentless as that truth, came the second wave of shock, harder and more jolting than the first. Kirsty was dying in pain—terrible pain. And she was somewhere on the other side of the world. In the Middle East . . . Syria, Lebanon, Israel?

Karen scrambled out of bed, compelled to move, to do something. She wrenched her mind out of shock and tried to grasp a line of purpose. Hold on, Kirsty! Hold on! I'll get there somehow. Please God, let her hold on. I've got to see her, be with her. She can't die yet.

Frantic eyes darted a glance at the clock. Two-seventeen. What could she do at this hour? It was the middle of the night. Ring the airport, get a seat. But to where? Where exactly was Kirsty?

The force of her need to reach her sister pushed back the panic that was scrambling

Karen's mind. An answer flashed into it. Kirsty was with Hal—Hal Chissolm—and Hal's father would know where they were. She ran out to the family room, snapping on the light switch as she flew past. She snatched the telephone book from the shelf below the kitchen bar. Her hands fumbled through the pages in desperate haste. Chissolm ... Chissolm ...

Her finger was running down the page when the sense of loss hit her. An awareness of pain shut off, a cold emptiness that glazed her eyes and froze her finger to the page. No ... no ... no! her mind screamed. You can't die like that! You can't! Not without me, Kirsty. Oh God, please ... please ... don't do that to Kirsty. Not Kirsty.

She shook her head, refusing to believe. It wasn't happening. It hadn't happened. It was only a nightmare—it had to be. But she could not dispel the dreadful certainty. Kirsty was dead.

No use questioning it; no use doubting it. The knowledge was there in the loneliness of her mind, in the emptiness of her heart. The togetherness she had known all her life, the special togetherness that only identical twins knew and shared, was gone.

Why had it happened? Why? Kirsty was so young, so vital. The need to know drove Karen's finger on down the page. Owen Chissolm could find out faster than anyone; he had the power and the contacts. She found the number and dialled. It was an agonising length of time before her call was answered, and then she could barely drag out the necessary words.

'My name is Karen Aylward and I'm Kirsty Balfour's sister. I need to speak to Mr Owen Chissolm, please.'

'I'm sorry, madam, Mr Chissolm is unavailable. If you would telephone the television studio after nine o'clock, his secretary . . .'

Unavailable. The word rang hollowly around Karen's mind. 'I have to speak to him!' she cried in protest.

'I'm sorry, madam, that's not possible,' came the firm reply. 'If you'd like to leave a message . . .'

What could she say? If she blurted out that Kirsty was dead they would think it was a crank call. Impossible to explain how she knew. And no one was going to wake Owen Chissolm up at this hour of the night to deal with a crank call. It was futile even trying. Everything was futile. There was nothing she could do to help Kirsty now.

A raw, primitive cry broke from her throat as she put the telephone down. She wrapped her arms around her chest, holding in, wildly clinging on, every instinct clawing to keep what had been lost. Come back . . . come back . . . come back . . . The mindless chant went on and on and she rocked herself in time to it. A beat of terrible need, unanswered.

Tears streamed down her cheeks, but her

chest was tight with an agony that no tears could expel. She couldn't bear it—couldn't bear the loss, the loneliness, the emptiness, the pain. Nothing in her life had been as bad as this, not even the death of their parents. She and Kirsty had still had each other then. And when Barry had walked out on her marriage, it was Kirsty who had supported her then too. But Kirsty wasn't with her any more, and never would be again.

Karen had no awareness of walking through the house to David's room. The need to hold someone was compelling. Gently she lifted the bed-covers away from his body and picked him up, hugging him closely, cradling him against her shoulder as she wrapped a blanket around him.

'Mummy . . .' he complained drowsily.

She forced out soothing words. 'Hush, darling, it's all right. Mummy's got you.'

She carried him over to the rocking-chair and sat down. He snuggled around on her lap until he settled comfortably. The softness and warmth of his beautiful little body and the gentle rise and fall of his breathing somehow eased the pain of her loss to a tolerable level. But the tears kept coming, welling out of the black chasm which Kirsty had left behind.

And rage swelled out of Karen's grief. Why had Kirsty died? Where had Hal been when Kirsty had needed help? Why hadn't he been there to save her? And with all the force of her devastating loss a wave of hatred crested the rage. Six years Kirsty had given him, loving him and sharing his life, but Hal Chissolm had never offered her any protection or security. A man who loved a woman should look after her. The only permanence Kirsty had got from him was death. Damn him! Damn him to hell!

Karen's feet automatically set the chair rocking. This was how she had nursed David to sleep when he was a new baby, and in the same way she had nursed him through hurts and upsets and sickness for three years. So now she nursed him through the long, dark hours of her grief, taking back from him the comfort she had always given.

Kirsty was dead, but Karen kept her alive in her mind, remembering. The daredevil tomboy, game for all manner of scrapes ... the schoolgirl stirring rebellion for the fun of it ... the university student throwing herself into every worthy cause on campus ... the globe-trotting reporter who had to be where it was all happening ... her exciting sister, her adventurous sister, her beloved sister.

Some time before dawn Karen's tears dried up. Her body was stiff from sitting in the one position and her arms ached from holding the child so closely to her. But she rocked on until the light of morning filtered through the curtains. Then quietly and smoothly she laid David back into his bed and walked out of his room. To stand alone.

She wondered if she could get some news from a radio station or a newspaper office, but common sense told her that Owen Chissolm would get the facts first. Hal would report back home, she thought bitterly, as the hatred surged back, gorging her throat. Hal Chissolm, the headline-maker, sending his stories back to Australia from all the trouble spots in the world. Kirsty would probably only be another headline to him—the hard, callous bastard!

Nine o'clock would come soon enough. She would wait. And she would insist on speaking to Owen Chissolm personally. After all, he was Kirsty's employer—had been Kirsty's employer, Karen corrected herself, gritting her teeth as another wave of grief hit her.

She dragged her feet out to the kitchen, made herself a cup of coffee and switched on the radio. She sat on the stool at the breakfast bar, her ears filtering out the music and the announcer's breakfast banter. She felt a vast, numb emptiness, but her mind was alert to any mention of the Middle East. There was none, not in the six o'clock or the seven o'clock news. She would have to stir herself shortly, ring the pre-school kindergarten and say she wouldn't be there today. Impossible to even think of going to work.

'Boo!'

Karen's head jerked up.

David giggled in triumph and ran to her for his morning kiss. Much to his delight she picked him up and whirled him around. Then she hugged him so hard he complained she was squeezing him.

'That's what you get for frightening me,' she chided, blinking back a stinging prickle of tears before loosening her embrace.

David's grin was full of playful mischief. 'I got you that time, didn't I, Mummy?'

'You surely did,' she agreed, loving him with a fierce mother-love.

He was so beautiful, with all the little-boy zest for life; always on the go, asking endless questions, wanting to see and hear and experience everything. He filled Karen's life, giving it a sense of satisfaction and achievement that no career could ever match. She had often worried whether Kirsty had ever regretted her decision to renounce motherhood. It was something that Karen would never know now.

'I'm thirsty,' David informed her, wriggling to be set free.

Karen put him down. 'Milk or orange juice?'

'Juice.'

'Say please.'

'Please,' he repeated with a funny wrinkle of his nose.

Karen shook her head warningly. Sometimes she suspected that David was deliberately forgetful about his manners—as if he was playing a teasing game with her, or testing her out to see how far he could go. She smiled down at him as he downed his orange juice. She wished, quite savagely, he had not inherited his father's eyes. They were so distinctive, such a clear, silvery grey and thickly lashed. Other mothers had told Karen they were wasted on a boy. Except for that one feature he was her son through and through, even to the chestnut gleam in his brown hair.

'Is it painting today, Mummy?'

A bleakness cut through Karen's maternal thoughts. Today was not like every other day. Today was the first day of her life without Kirsty. 'We're not going to kindergarten today, David. We're going to play at home instead. You can paint if you like. Now let's go and get dressed, and then we'll have breakfast.'

David chattered on, oblivious to the dark emptiness in Karen's soul. Karen dressed him in his best play-clothes. For herself she chose a brown gaberdine skirt and a beige silk shirt. She pulled on a pair of tights and slid her feet into low-heeled, fashionable shoes. Her mind was assessing the possibilities as she brushed her thick, shoulder-length hair. She might have to go to the television studio. She had to see someone, do something positive.

'Are we going out?' asked David, eyeing her clothes hopefully.

The question was not unreasonable—usually Karen wore jeans around the house. She put down her hairbrush and took his hand. 'Perhaps. Ready for breakfast now? Would you like banana on your cornflakes?'

'Mmmh. Please.' He beamed at her to emphasise the 'please'.

A smile tugged at her mouth as he broke away to run ahead of her. He was so alive—and could very easily become a cheeky little brat if she let him get away with too much.

He had climbed up on to her stool and picked a banana out of the fruit bowl by the time Karen reached the kitchen. He handed it to her and then set himself down at his own little table in the family room. It had been the breakfast room when Karen had been married to Barry, but she had cleared it to make a good play area for David. It was the brightest, sunniest room in the house. Most of David's toys resided in its cupboards and the walls were decorated with his artistic efforts. It also adjoined the kitchen, which made it handy for Karen to keep an eye on him when she was cooking.

She set his cornflakes in front of him and was intending to go and telephone the kindergarten when the doorbell shrilled its summons. Karen's heart contracted as her gaze lifted to the wall-clock. Seven fifty-two. Five and a half hours. Would it be someone about Kirsty?

'David, I have to answer the door. Eat your breakfast and then play with your building blocks. Okay?' she said quickly, struggling to keep her voice steady and natural.

He nodded, his mouth already full of cornflakes.

Karen shut the family room door behind her.

David could open it by standing on his chair, but she wanted to discourage any impulsive move to follow her. It would be easier if he did not overhear anything about Kirsty's death. She would tell him in her own good time.

Be calm and dignified, she told herself sternly. The how and the why of Kirsty's death could not alter that fact. Just accept the news and find out what had to be done. She took a deep breath and opened the door with decisive swiftness.

She saw the shock in his eyes even while she fought to recover her own. Hal's father, Owen Chissolm himself. The media magnate's face was too well publicised for her to be mistaken, though this morning it seemed an older face, strained and grey-looking.

Incredulity and a flicker of hope chased across his eyes. It took Karen a moment to realise what he was thinking ... that Kirsty was alive and well, standing there right in front of him. He was seeing her mirror-image; the thick, straight chestnut hair; the wide hazel eyes; the eyebrows with their offset arch; smooth, creamy skin, and the chin with the slight dimple ... all the features that belonged to Kirsty Balfour.

'I'm Karen Aylward, Mr Chissolm. Kirsty's sister,' she stated firmly.

He lifted a hand that trembled to his face. It was a curiously vulnerable gesture from such a powerful man. 'Forgive me. For some reason I had surmised you were a younger sister. I had no idea you were identical twins.'

Karen felt a twinge of compassion for him; he had shouldered an unenviable task. His hand dropped to his side and his shoulders squared into a stiff, dignified bearing. The pale blue eyes were washed with pain, but they met hers unflinchingly.

'I've come to see you about your sister. Please, may I come in?'

'Yes, of course.'

He frowned as he stepped inside. 'Is your husband home as well?'

Karen shut the door and turned to find Owen Chissolm looking distinctly ill at ease. 'I have no husband now, Mr Chissolm. We were divorced two years ago,' she said quietly.

Before she turned away to lead him into the living room, Karen got the oddest impression that Owen Chissolm had felt relief to learn that there was no husband. Which seemed absurd. Karen shrugged off the idea; it was irrelevant.

'Please sit down.' She gestured to an armchair and seated herself on the sofa. Although she knew what was coming her nerves were stretched taut with the effort to stay composed.

Owen Chissolm did not sit down. He was a big man, over six feet tall and bulky. He wore a dark pin-striped suit, a white shirt and a red, grey and navy tie. His sombre clothes and the greyish tinge to his face robbed him of his much-vaunted colourful personality. He had

been handsome in his youth, probably more
handsome than his son. He could still be called
striking with his strong features and thick,
snow-white hair. But he looked old this
morning, old and sick and tired. He made a
stiff, uneasy gesture.

'I don't come with good news, Mrs Aylward.'

She held his gaze steadily. 'I know. You don't
have to break it gently. I know Kirsty is dead,
Mr Chissolm. I don't expect you to understand,
but I . . . I felt her die early this morning. I tried
to contact you then, but I was told you were
unavailable. I would appreciate it if you'd just
give me the facts.' Even as she spoke, Karen
had to fight the grief she was controlling so
rigidly.

Owen Chissolm stared at her for a long
moment before he sat down. He sank back into
the chair and passed a hand across his forehead
as if clearing his mind. 'It was a terrorist bomb.
Not directed at anyone in particular, planted in
a parked car across from the hotel where your
sister . . .'

He paused and cleared his throat. So far he
had recited the facts quietly and calmly but his
voice shook a little as he continued. '. . . where
your sister . . . and my son . . . were staying in
Tel Aviv. Kirsty and Hal were leaving to go out
for dinner. They'd just passed through the
doors to the street. Kirsty was slightly ahead of
Hal. She . . .'

'He's alive!' Karen could not control the

surge of bitterness that drove her to her feet. 'He's alive and Kirsty is dead. She was in front of him and she took the brunt of the explosion, didn't she?'

Owen Chissolm displayed no emotion. 'As far as I know my son is still alive, Mrs Aylward. A team of surgeons have been operating on him for some three hours now. There's a slight chance that he might live.'

Karen turned away, regretting her outburst. Her hatred of Hal Chissolm was shot into fragments by the realisation of his father's pain. Shame burnt scorching heat into her cheeks. 'I'm sorry,' she muttered, and dropped back on to the sofa. She stared down at her hands for a few fraught moments until suitable words formed in her mind. 'It was good of you to visit me personally when you must be . . . so worried. I hope the operation is successful.' She sucked in a deep breath and plunged on. 'Can you tell me what I should do about . . . about Kirsty?'

He did not answer. She glanced up to find a strange mixture of compassion and determination in his expression. 'Your sister lived for several minutes after the explosion.'

The memory of the pain and the frantic futility of those few minutes shadowed Karen's eyes. 'I know.'

Owen Chissolm cleared his throat, obviously discomfited by a knowledge he didn't understand. 'Mrs Aylward, Kirsty died in Hal's arms. She was able to speak to him before she died.'

He paused, seemingly uncertain as to how best to continue. 'Even if Hal survives this operation, the doctors have warned that various complications can arise. He'll be on the critical list for some time. I've come to ask you to grant my son's most urgent request. Possibly his last request.'

The look in his eyes . . . the question . . . Suddenly Karen's stomach curled into knots.

'Hal wants to see his son.'

No! No, no, no! The scream rocketed around Karen's brain. Other questions darted into it. Why, Kirsty? Why did you tell him? It was a sacred trust between us. You vowed secrecy. Never to tell—anyone, ever.

Owen Chissolm's eyes were boring into her, watching, waiting. 'Kirsty told him before she died that they had a son, and the boy was with you.'

'David is my son now, Mr Chissolm,' Karen stated with all the fierce possessiveness of a mother. 'Not Kirsty's, not Hal's. Mine.' She held his hard gaze with an unwavering hardness of her own.

'How old is the boy?'

'That's immaterial!' she retorted vehemently. Her hands were shaking and she clenched them into tight fists.

Owen Chissolm studied her for a long time before choosing his next words, and when he spoke it was with surprising gentleness. 'Mrs Aylward, I have no intention of trying to take

the child away from you. I simply want you and
the boy to fly with me to Tel Aviv as soon as it
can be organised—today if possible. Whatever
the cost. Hal is my only son and I . . .'

The slight falter in his voice was firmly
corrected. 'I'll pay anything to do what I can for
him. Once we're there you can decide what you
want done about your sister. I'll make myself
responsible for any arrangements you'd like
carried out. If Hal is still alive, I would ask you
to visit the hospital with me and show him . . .
the boy. That's all I ask. I believe you can
understand my desire to give my son anything
that can help him at such a time as this.'

He heaved a sigh and the sickness was back
in his eyes. 'I apologise, very sincerely, for
intruding on your privacy and your grief. I
appreciate that I have no right to ask so much
of you. I can only appeal to you . . . beg you to
come with me.'

'No!' Fear left no room for compassion. She
couldn't do it. It would be admitting that David
was Hal's son, and she would never do that.
Not for any reason.

'Kirsty wanted Hal to know he had a son,
Mrs Aylward. It was her dying wish. Can you
ignore that?'

No, she couldn't. Tears blurred her eyes. She
did not understand why Kirsty had betrayed
her. Perhaps her sister had believed that Hal
was dying too and she had wanted him to know
they were leaving a life behind . . . a son born of

both of them. A son who had been handed over to Karen a few days after Kirsty had given birth. As much as Karen recoiled from Owen Chissolm's proposition, as much as she hated Hal Chissolm, she owed Kirsty too much to refuse her last wish. She owed her David.

'Just once, then. I'll go, and I'll take David. But I'll only show him to Hal one time. No more than that,' she choked out despairingly, admitting nothing, yet knowing that her acceptance was a tacit admission.

'That decision is up to you, Mrs Aylward. I will not press you further.'

Tears rolled down her cheeks. 'He's my son,' she whispered, her eyes imploring him for more assurance. Would adoption papers stand up against the might of the Chissolm family? Would she lose David too? Surely the law would be on her side.

Owen Chissolm climbed to his feet and stepped over to the sofa. He took Karen's hands and gently pulled her up. Still holding her hands and looking her straight in the eye, he spoke with a firmness which steadied her. 'I promise you that you won't lose anything by coming with me. But we have to move quickly or it could be too late.

'Leave it to me, I'll get everything organised. Pack whatever clothes you think you'll need, and be ready to leave this afternoon. I'll keep you posted on developments.'

She wanted to ask . . . what if Hal died before

they left? But it didn't matter. Owen Chissolm knew about David now. Hal had never wanted a child, wouldn't want it at this late date either. It was his father who was the danger.

'Before I go, may I . . .' He paused, seeing the flare of fear in her eyes. 'May I see your son, Mrs Aylward?'

'He's . . . he's playing. I don't want him to be upset.'

'Trust me.'

Could she trust him? She had little choice now. She had to. With a sigh of reluctant resignation she led the way to the family room, where David was sitting on the carpet, constructing what was undoubtedly another space station, his little face screwed into concentrated purpose as he pressed one more block on to the top of his impressive edifice. Then he lifted his face and beamed at her, but with barely a pause his gaze slid to the man behind her.

'Visitor, Mummy?'

'Yes. Say hello to Mr Chissolm, David.'

David pushed himself to his feet, his face lit with welcome. 'Hello, Mr Chiss . . .'

'Mr Chissolm,' Karen prompted.

'Mr Chissolm,' he repeated triumphantly.

The old man crouched down beside him and Karen saw the years and the greyness fade from the formidable face as he looked into David's eyes . . . Hal's eyes. 'Hello, David. What are you building?'

'A space station.'

'Looks fantastic. Have you ever flown in a big jet aeroplane, David?'

'No.'

'How about we go flying tonight? You and Mummy and me. Would you like that?'

David's eyes widened with excitement. 'Can we, Mummy? Can we?'

Karen nodded, fighting the prick of tears. What chance did she have against the wealth and power of Owen Chissolm?

'And since we're going flying together, I'd like you to call me Pop instead of Mr Chissolm.'

'Pop.' David beamed at him. 'That's easy. Is that your first name?'

'For you it is. Now why don't you build a jet plane to show me when I come back later today?'

'All right,' David agreed quickly, dropping to his knees to get started on it.

Owen Chissolm patted the small head in approval as he straightened up. If there had been any doubt in his mind, there was none now. He had just acknowledged his grandson.

Karen turned away, heartsick and frightened. She walked to the front door, all too aware of the powerful man following her. He had given his word that he would not attempt to take David away from her, and she had to believe it. She held the door open for him, wanting him gone, wishing he had never come, knowing there was no escape from him now. He might not take David from her but no way was he going to leave them alone. The Owen Chissolms of this world jealously guarded their flesh-and-blood heirs.

He paused by her. 'He's a fine boy.'

She lifted proud, defiant eyes. 'He's my son.'

'He's also Hal's. And Kirsty's.'

It was a flat, unequivocal statement. He walked away without another word. A chauffeur opened the passenger door of the Rolls Royce standing at the kerb and Owen Chissolm stepped in without looking back. He disappeared behind the tinted windows of his status-symbol car and was driven away.

Mission accomplished, Karen thought bitterly. And where would it all end? She closed her eyes and thought of Kirsty lying in Hal Chissolm's arms, choking out her last, fatal words. What had been in her mind? Not this. Surely not this.

CHAPTER TWO

'GOOD morning. This is your captain speaking. We will be landing at Lydda Airport in fifteen minutes . . .'

Lydda Airport . . . Tel Aviv . . . the city of Kirsty's death. The long hours of travel had added their weight to the depression that darkened Karen's soul. Her tired eyes caught the tense strain on Owen Chissolm's face. Perhaps it was worse for him, she thought with a twinge of compassion. Hal had survived the operation, but Owen did not know what news would be waiting for him. They had been in the air for some twenty hours and his son's condition had been described as critical.

Despite her fear of Owen Chissolm's position and power, Karen had found that she could not dislike the man. To her he had been all kindness and consideration, and with David he had been patience itself throughout the long journey. Although every instinct told her to keep him at as far a distance as possible, Owen Chissolm was gradually moving in on her and David, and she did not know how to fight him. David was completely won over by 'Pop' already, basking in his grandfather's attention.

24

Owen Chissolm was renowned for his take-overs, Karen thought despondently.

'Karen . . .'

She glanced warily at him. The pale blue eyes probed hers with some urgency.

'I'm sorry, but I must speak now—there's so little time left. I understand and sympathise with your grief for your sister, but I must consider Hal. You don't like him, do you?'

It seemed callous to admit it in the face of his pain. 'I've never met your son, Mr Chissolm,' she said evasively. 'I only know of him through Kirsty.'

'Please be frank with me. I'll be honest and say there've been times when I haven't liked him myself. But you showed hatred, Karen, and that isn't related to the death of your sister.'

She hesitated, then blurted out the truth. 'He robbed Kirsty of the happiness she should have had. Because of his selfishness, he deprived Kirsty of keeping her own child. I can never forgive him for that.'

'So you hate him.'

'Yes.'

His face tightened. 'Human beings are never black and white, Karen. You've never met my son, yet you've made a harsh judgement of him. Hal and I haven't always seen eye to eye, but he is my son and I love him. He may be dying. I'm asking you to act with some forebearance when you see Hal. I hope you and I can be reasonable people . . . in an unreasonable situation.'

Her whole being cringed in revulsion at the thought of seeing Hal at all, let alone showing David to him, but she had to fulfil Kirsty's last wish. 'I'll try to be reasonable,' she answered shortly.

David stirred from his sleep. 'Mummy . . . my ears are hurting.'

The plane had begun its descent. Karen showed David how to ease the pressure in his ears by holding his nose and trying to blow through it. She then pointed to the view from his window to distract him from his discomfort. The descent seemed to take forever and it was a relief when the bump of wheels on the tarmac heralded their arrival.

All discomfort was quickly forgotten as David became totally absorbed in the workings of an international airport. Karen walked silently and wearily beside Owen Chissolm, grateful for his guidance through foreign territory. Despite the length of their journey, it was only mid-morning. Added to her physical fatigue and emotional exhaustion, the time-lag made her feel completely disorientated.

Inside the terminal they were joined by Owen Chissolm's valet, Harper, who had travelled business class. Apart from the introduction before they had boarded the plane, Karen had not seen or spoken to him.

Two Israelis came forward to greet them. They spoke English as well as Hebrew. The latest information on Hal was that he was still on the critical list, but he had regained consciousness a couple of times, asking repeatedly for his son. He had been assured that both his father and his son were on their way.

Apparently no mention had been made of Kirsty's sister, Karen thought resentfully. As far as Hal was concerned she was irrelevant. But he would soon find out differently. The news seemed to act as a tonic on Owen Chissolm; he brightened visibly and his step became more spry. Karen was glad, for his father's sake, that Hal was still alive, but the knowledge sharpened the pain of her own loss. Why couldn't Kirsty have only been injured? Why did her sister have to die?

'Karen . . .'

She lifted bleak, grieving eyes to Owen Chissolm.

He hesitated, torn between his own sense of urgency and the realisation of what this city meant to her. But urgency won. 'Harper will be taking our luggage to the hotel. I'm going straight to the hospital. I know it's asking a great deal of you, but we've come this far now and . . .'

'I'll come with you.' Better to get it over with, she thought in grim resignation. Then she could give her complete attention to doing something about Kirsty.

Apology and gratitude were in the gentle squeeze of her arm. 'It may be a long wait at the hospital,' Owen Chissolm warned kindly.

Karen looked down at David and knew there would be no peace for her until she had shown him to Hal. 'We'll manage.'

A limousine was waiting for them. One of the Israelis took the front passenger seat next to the driver, while Owen Chissolm sat in the back with Karen and David. He was certainly efficient, Karen thought ruefully. When he moved, he moved with style, everything pulling together like clockwork. Power and wealth were never ignored.

Tears swam into her eyes, tears of fatigue and helplessness and rage against the situation. She had lost Kirsty; would the Chissolms take David from her too? The adoption had been legalised, so the law was surely on her side but the fact that she was a single, working mother might go against her. If only Barry had stayed with her she would be in a much stronger position.

'Why didn't you have any children of your own, Karen? There must have been a reason.'

The question startled her, coming as it did on top of her own thoughts of Barry. She cast Owen Chissolm a bleak look. 'My husband couldn't father children. Unlike your son, he was infertile.'

The blue eyes were sharp now and they held hers intently. 'And he couldn't cope with the problem.'

The soft statement rattled a host of painful memories. That fatal medical report had been the death-knell on their marriage. Barry had started playing around to prove something about his manhood and Karen had felt doubly cheated. 'Neither of us coped with it very well. We'd been trying to have a baby for four years,' she admitted sadly.

'But he was still with you when David came along.'

Karen glanced quickly at David, but the little boy was too busy looking out the car window to take any heed of the conversation. She shot a warning frown at Owen Chissolm and answered in a low tone, 'Yes, he was still with me. After a rather shattering year I persuaded Barry into putting our names down to ... for a baby. Then Kirsty became pregnant. She said Hal would suggest an abortion and she couldn't do that. She wanted us to bring up the child. But when he was ours, Barry couldn't bear my loving a child that was not his own and I wouldn't give the baby up. So we parted.'

'Then David was indirectly responsible for the break-up of your marriage,' Owen Chissolm mused quietly. 'And now he's become your whole life.'

Karen's jaw tightened with determination. 'David is my son, Mr Chissolm—legally, morally, and in every other way. And no one is going to take him away from me. Nor will I ever give him up.'

He met her defiant gaze with a sympathy

that Karen had not expected and he answered her in a calm, soothing voice. 'No one is asking you to, Karen. I will say this, in justice to my son—Hal was given no choice in the matter. He didn't know about David until Kirsty told him. Don't condemn him unheard.'

Unheard! Karen gritted her teeth against saying any more, but her mind seethed with a scornful rejection of Owen Chissolm's argument. Actions spoke louder than words, and Kirsty wouldn't have given up her baby if Hal had even suggested he might like fatherhood. If his life wasn't in danger now he wouldn't be wanting to bother with David. It was no strain to look at a little boy; that didn't require a choice of life-styles. She kept a grim silence for the rest of the way to the hospital.

The vast medical complex was another novelty to David. Owen Chissolm and the Israeli man went to consult with doctors while Karen and David remained in a visitors' lounge. Karen felt weak from fatigue and apprehension, and sick with thoughts of her sister; the hospital reminded her too forcibly of death. David's questions grew more and more difficult to answer as they waited for news. It seemed an interminable age before Owen Chissolm returned.

He sank on to the seat next to Karen, his face drawn into grave lines, his eyes deeply anxious. 'Karen, Hal is conscious now. I've told him . . . prepared him . . . but I'm not sure he understands that . . .' He faltered and shook his head. 'He might think that you're Kirsty—God knows I did at first. Can you handle that, Karen?'

The blood drained from her face. 'You can't mean that you want me to pretend . . .'

'No, of course not,' he cut in quickly. 'Just . . . be ready. I realise how distressing this must be for you and I didn't want you further upset by something beyond my control. It might be easier, on everyone, if you let me take David . . .'

'No!' Her eyes flared defiance as she stood up and stiffened her spine. 'We go together or not at all,' she declared adamantly, and to further emphasise the point, she stepped over to David who was leafing through the magazines on a nearby table, and took his hand.

Owen Chissolm rose to his feet. 'It's not good, Karen. Not for him or for you.'

'David is my only consideration. It would frighten him to be separated from me in a foreign place. Hospitals are frightening enough to adults, let alone children,' she argued, not caring if she was being unreasonable. No one was going to take her son away from her—no one!

Owen Chissolm gestured an appeal, then dropped his hand in the face of her obduracy. 'I'll take you to his room,' he shrugged.

'Where are we going now?' asked David as they began walking.

'To visit someone who wants to meet you,' Karen answered cautiously. 'But he's very sick, so you must be very good and quiet.'

'Who is he?'

'He's Mr Chissolm's son. Like you're my son.'

'Is he like me, Pop?' David asked in all his childish innocence, and Karen's heart turned over.

Owen Chissolm answered matter-of-factly. 'Yes, like you, David. Except he's grown up.'

'What's his name?'

The questions and answers continued all the way to Hal's room, but Karen barely heard them. She was steeling herself to face the man who had been Kirsty's lover—and the father of her son. The biological father, she reminded herself savagely. He was no more than that, and no matter that he was at death's door, she would feel no pity for him. Kirsty was dead.

All the primitive instincts of a mother impelled Karen to stoop and pick David up as Owen Chissolm opened Hal's door. She clutched him to her possessively, and her eyes defied Owen Chissolm and the whole damned world. Kirsty's dying words had brought them here, but Karen was not going to let Hal or his father dictate anything. Owen Chissolm made no comment. He pushed the door wide open, stepped inside and waved her to enter. Karen propped David on to her hip and holding him there very firmly, walked into the room.

Hal's eyes were shut, his face was still and drawn and pale. Karen swallowed hard to ease a sudden constriction in her throat. It flashed through her mind that she did not want him to die. Death was so useless, so final. Doubts stabbed into her heart. What if the shock of seeing her . . . seeing the living, mirror-image of Kirsty . . .

'Is he asleep?' whispered David.

The eyes opened. Silvery grey eyes—David's eyes. But full of a pain and knowledge that no little boy's eyes could ever project. It was too late for Karen to retreat now. Those eyes held her pinned. They clung to her for a long, spine-chilling moment before moving to David. They drank in every detail of the child in her arms, but there was no joy in the slow, thorough appraisal. It was a torture to both him and Karen.

'Hello.'

He flinched at David's impulsive greeting, as if it hurt him, then the grey eyes sharpened into a more concentrated focus.

'What are those things in your arm?' asked David, his curiosity getting the better of the instructions from his mother.

'They're called drips, David,' Owen Chissolm explained quietly and calmly. 'Hal is too sick to eat and those tubes drip liquid food into his body so he'll get stronger.'

'Can I see?' David struggled to get down.

Karen let him go. The man in the bed was no

threat to her. Owen Chissolm caught David's
hand and led him around to the other side of the
bed, while Hal's eyes followed them. Owen
lifted David up to show him the drips.

'Do they hurt?' he asked Hal.

'No.' It was barely a whisper. A spasm of
pain crossed his face. 'David.' The name was
pushed out, an explosion of breath which held a
note of despair.

David's curiosity was piqued. 'What's in
them? It's not milk or orange juice.'

Owen Chissolm answered him.

Hal slowly rolled his head back towards
Karen and the grey eyes were dark pools of
torment. 'Karen . . .' It was not a question but
an affirmation of her identity. Not Kirsty . . .
Karen. 'You had him? All the time?'

'Yes,' she answered huskily, too choked up to
project a firm voice. She had not anticipated
this reaction from him. Somehow he wasn't the
Hal Chissolm she had envisaged. His pain and
despair were too real for her to ignore . . . too
immediate to brush aside. This was not a man
whose ego had demanded the presence of a son,
but a man who seemed tortured by what he had
missed.

'Why didn't she tell me?'

The harsh croak carried a note of accusation
that hardened Karen's heart against him.
Loyalty to her sister demanded it. 'Kirsty did
tell you—that's why we're here. And the
question you ask should be asked of yourself,'
she stated coldly.

Pain answered her. 'Do you think I haven't?' He dragged in a laboured breath. 'She knew me. She knew I wanted . . .'

'You got what you wanted!' Karen burst out fiercely. On a wave of bitter hostility she stalked around the bed and snatched David up into her arms. Her eyes were blind to the pain of the man in the bed; she could only think of her sister. 'Kirsty lived and died for you. She gave you herself. She didn't owe you anything. Nor does she owe you anything now.'

David began whimpering, bewildered and upset by his mother's angry words and actions. Karen pressed his head down on her shoulder and laid her cheek on his hair in automatic reassurance, but her eyes never left Hal's. She lowered her voice, but it shook with emotion as she delivered her last judgement.

'You've met my son. If Kirsty thought she owed you that much then I've now paid the debt. You have your life—be grateful for that. It's more than my sister has. And if you ever want to father children, Hal Chissolm, marry the woman first. Then she'll know that you want them!'

She turned her back on him and marched out of the room, fighting to contain the torrent of emotion churning through her. It was impossible. The accumulated grief and strain of the last two days burst into body-racking sobs as she closed the door behind her. She tottered a few steps down the corridor, tears pouring down her cheeks.

'Mummy . . .' David piped anxiously, winding his little arms tightly around her neck.

Karen couldn't answer, couldn't form words. She shook her head helplessly and hugged him to her heaving chest. Her knees buckled and she would have collapsed but for the strong support of an arm around her waist. Owen Chissolm pulled her against him for more solid bolstering. He made no attempt to take David from her, but held them both in his embrace, murmuring soothing words to David until Karen had wept all her tears.

'I'm sorry,' she choked out, guilt and shame weighing heavily on her heart. She hadn't meant to attack Hal like that, not when he was so weak and defenceless. If he died . . .

'My dear, I feel I'm the one who should be apologising. It was too much to ask of you. I'll take you to the hotel now and see that you and David are comfortably settled.'

But she could not accept that. 'Hal? What about . . .'

'Hal's like me, a fighter. I think you may have just given him the will to fight for his life.'

The assurance was strangely bitter-sweet, but Karen was too drained to question her feelings or the situation any further. She accepted the calm satisfaction in Owen Chissolm's voice and went with him, grateful to be able to lean on his strength. He was right: it was too much for her. Altogether too much.

CHAPTER THREE

THERE was something about walking along a beach that soothed the most despondent spirits. The wash of water upon sand held a timeless constancy that dwarfed everything else. Karen could almost forget she was in this foreign city which had taken her sister's life. But it was not Bondi or Manly Beach under her feet. The Mediterranean Sea did not have the rolling surf of the Pacific Ocean. And the water was warm.

The suite that Owen Chissolm had provided for her and David in the Hilton Hotel was spacious and luxurious, but Karen did not feel comfortable in it. The breeze in her face and the sun on her back felt more like home. The beach was only a short walk from the hotel, and David had been pressing to play on it ever since he had spotted it from his bedroom window. Karen had promised the outing as a reward for his good behaviour during the long morning's ordeal of seeing to the official details of Kirsty's death.

Owen Chissolm had been as good as his word, helping her with the necessary forms, answering questions when she had been too distressed to speak and arranging a funeral service for Kirsty. Karen had felt compelled to

37

see the scene of her sister's death and they had driven along the fatal street, past the hotel where Hal and Kirsty had been staying. But there had been nothing to see, no sense of tragedy left behind. If windows had been broken, they had been replaced. Any damage to the street surrounds had been repaired. The marks of death and destruction had been erased as quickly as footsteps in the sand.

'Karen!'

It was Owen Chissolm's voice. She turned and waited for him to catch up to her, and David broke away from her handhold and ran to greet him. The old man smiled and bent to return the greeting, chatting indulgently to his grandson for a minute or two before resuming his approach to Karen. The sober business suit of this morning had been replaced by casual slacks and a knitted shirt, and he looked more friendly than formidable.

Karen no longer feared him. He had been kindness itself to her and she did not know how she would have coped without him this morning. She could not even summon up any resentment towards the growing affinity between grandfather and grandson. Owen Chissolm was a good man.

'You'll get your trousers wet, Pop,' David warned.

'Then I'd better walk on the other side of Mummy and leave the splashing to you.'

He fell into step beside Karen and David

happily resumed his water games. Karen knew that Owen Chissolm had been to the hospital again. It had been an enormous relief this morning when he had told her that his son had passed a peaceful night and seemed a little stronger. Even so, she still could not think of yesterday's encounter without shame.

She wished she had been more controlled, more dignified, and above all, more sympathetic to Hal's state of health. Even though she had only spoken the truth. If Hal had wanted children, he should have married Kirsty—to Karen's mind, that was a truth which exonerated Kirsty of having wronged Hal in any way.

'Is ... is everything all right?' she asked stiffly.

'Hal is holding his own, if that's what you're asking.'

'Yes.'

She felt his sharp glance at her but kept her own gaze averted. No matter how good Owen Chissolm had been to her she could not feel kindly towards his son.

'There is one thing. Hal wants to see you again, Karen,' Owen Chissolm stated softly.

She clenched her teeth against a bitter retort, then swung a hard, mocking gaze to the man beside her. 'You mean he wants to see David.'

Owen Chissolm shook his head and eyed her with discomfiting concern. 'No, he's seen David, Karen. One look was enough to prove he was the father of the boy. As it was for me. A

sick-room is no place for a child to be visiting.'
He paused and his voice softened to appeal. 'He
wants . . . needs . . . to talk to you, Karen.'

'What about?' she grated, barely hiding the
revulsion she felt at the thought of facing
Kirsty's lover again.

'I don't know—he didn't tell me. I would
assume that it's about David. Maybe Kirsty—I
don't know.'

Kirsty! No, she didn't want to hear anything
about Kirsty from Hal. She couldn't bear it.
The memory of the pain and despair in Hal's
eyes flashed into her mind and she thrust it
away. He couldn't really have loved Kirsty.
None of this would have happened if he had
done the right thing by her. He was selfish and
uncaring of anyone but himself.

'No, I won't go,' she said decisively. She had
fulfilled her part of the bargain she had made
with Owen Chissolm and even though she had
known from the beginning that there would be
more to it, she couldn't face that now. Not yet.
She lifted eyes which held a mute plea for
understanding. 'I'm sorry. It wouldn't do him
any good, you know—to Hal, I mean. I'd get
upset. I can't . . . I just can't feel . . . indifferent
to him.'

'You haven't given him much of a chance,
Karen,' Owen Chissolm pointed out gently. He
sighed and offered her a commiserating little
smile. 'But it's been a very grim day for you.
Perhaps you'll give it some thought.'

She didn't want to think about it but she nodded. If Hal lived she would have to see him soon enough. His reaction yesterday indicated that he would want access to David.

'Are there any special flowers you would like me to order for the service tomorrow?'

Tears stung Karen's eyes. Flowers—a wreath for Kirsty. Grief welled up again and she shook her head dumbly. She would do it herself when she went back to the hotel.

'I've had Kirsty's suitcase of belongings put in your room, Karen,' Owen Chissolm added gently, and handed her a sealed envelope. 'This was given to me this morning and I've held it back until now because you looked so distressed. Kirsty was wearing it.'

Karen knew what it was before she tore the envelope open and the fine gold chain with the little jade bird fell into her hand. Kirsty had bought it in Hong Kong, along with the little jade koala bear which hung around Karen's neck—their twenty-first birthday presents. 'This is me, as free as a bird,' Kirsty had declared gaily, 'and you're as lovable as a koala.' They had always worn them, another link between them. And suddenly Karen knew what flowers to buy. Strelitzia ... Bird of Paradise ... with the blue of the sky for a freewheeling bird and the fiery gold of Kirsty's wild spirit. Tears spilled down Karen's cheeks and there was nothing she could do to stop them.

Owen Chissolm gave her arm a gentle squeeze. 'I'll take David for a walk to the end of the breakwater—he can watch the fishermen for a while. All right, Karen?'

She nodded. He was good with David, drawing him smoothly away to give her time to recover. He was good to her too. Maybe she should see Hal, Karen thought miserably, if only to repay Owen Chissolm some of his kindness. The thought persisted at the back of her mind, a twinge of guilt which not even her grief for Kirsty could dispel.

She had regained her composure by the time they returned. David was full of chatter about the little drummer fish he had seen being caught. Owen Chissolm accompanied them back to the hotel and had dinner with them before he took his leave for another visit to the hospital. He did not press Karen for a change of mind on Hal's request, but she was very conscious of the refusal he would be taking to his son. She felt mean, and she didn't like the feeling.

She did not sleep well. The next morning Owen Chissolm arrived at her door with an armful of parcels. 'Toys for David. I hope you don't mind, but they should keep him amused while we're away at the funeral service.'

Karen could not object. Again Owen Chissolm had thought of everything. Harper, his valet, had been assigned to baby-sit, and he arrived while David was still tearing open parcels in wide-eyed excitement. Harper had been very helpful in getting her and David settled into their rooms at the hotel, and he was a kindly man, very correct and polite, but with a gentle warmth in his manner which was automatically endearing.

Short and rotund, he was impeccably dressed as befitted a valet, and his sparse, greying hair was carefully combed over his balding crown. Gold-rimmed spectacles dominated what was an otherwise bland face and he looked far too formal to squat on the floor with David, but he proceeded to do so, apparently quite prepared to play with him.

Karen gave him a few practical instructions which he assured her would be carried out. David made no fuss about her leaving him; he was too entranced with his new toys. Karen wondered wryly if a child could be easily bought, then discarded the thought. Owen Chissolm was not trying to buy David. And Hal? Only God knew what Hal would do about David in the future. But maybe she should see him, if only to find out.

Ever since she had woken up Karen had tried not to think about Kirsty's funeral, but she could no longer push it from the forefront of her mind as she left the hotel with Owen Chissolm. She wore a dark forest-green dress, not black. Kirsty had always hated black. Green was her favourite colour, just as it was Karen's. So

many likes and dislikes they had shared. But no
more. Not any more.

The service was brief—too brief for the wide-
roaming life Kirsty had led, Karen thought
sadly. The burial was even more of an ordeal.
Karen clung on to Owen Chissolm's arm,
feeling even more bereft than she had done on
the night Kirsty had died. This was the end,
and the love she had always felt for her sister
was a heavy burden on her heart. It desperately
needed some expression.

And Karen thought of Hal. Kirsty had loved
Hal. It did not matter what Karen herself
thought of him, Kirsty had loved him. And Hal
wanted to see her. Maybe Kirsty would have
wanted her to go to him. It was something she
could do for her beloved sister.

'Does Hal still want to see me?' she asked
Owen Chissolm on the drive back to the hotel.

'Yes,' he answered briefly.

'I'll visit him tonight, after David's gone to
bed. Would Harper baby-sit again?'

'Yes, of course.' He reached across and
pressed her hand. 'You're a good woman,
Karen. Thank you.'

She wanted to say she was doing it for Kirsty,
but the lump in her throat was too large to
circumvent.

Her resolve wavered several times during
that long afternoon. David required little of her
attention. He was absorbed in his new collec-
tion of toys, particularly the Lego set which

enabled him to build a great variety of interesting structures. She wished she knew why Kirsty had told Hal about David. She could feel the future shifting from the foundations she had laid for herself and David, and it filled her with too many frightening uncertainties.

Owen Chissolm joined them for dinner in their suite. Apart from saying that Hal seemed a little stronger, he did not talk about his son. David, of course, was full of all that he'd been doing and the conversation centred on him. Karen did not feel like talking at all; every minute increased her anxiety about tonight's meeting with Hal. Finally it was time to settle David into bed, and for once there was no argument from him. He was asleep almost before he hit the pillow.

Harper arrived to baby-sit, armed with a book and a reassuring smile, but Karen was too tense to smile back at him. Before her courage could desert her, she took her leave with Owen Chissolm. Hal's father had become a source of comfort and strength to her in the last couple of days. For his sake as well as Kirsty's, she was determined to control her animosity towards Hal tonight.

They were almost at the hospital when Owen Chissolm spoke about the forthcoming visit. 'Karen, I hope you don't mind, but Hal wants to see you alone.'

Alone! What did he want to say to her that he

didn't want his father to hear? Karen's tension wound up another notch. 'Where will you be?' she asked.

'I'll take you up to his room, then wait for you in the lounge on the first floor, where you waited with David last time. Unless you want me to . . .'

'No, that's all right,' she said quickly. Whatever Hal had to say she would meet with equanimity—as far as possible. She could always walk out of his room; he was not in a position to stop her. But she would try very hard to give him a fair hearing.

Karen held on to that resolution right up to the moment that Owen Chissolm let her into Hal's room. The first shock was the change in Hal's appearance. Gone was the stubble of beard and the grey shadow of death. The clean-shaven face still looked pale and drawn, but the eyes which met Karen's held no weakness; they were hard and cold and challenging. This was the man she had imagined him to be. Even confined to a hospital bed he emanated a ruthless strength which was unnerving.

The thick black hair had been neatly combed to frame his angular face. He had a high, wide brow and high cheekbones which emphasised the large, deeply-set eyes. His jawline sloped to a strong, chiselled chin. The full-lipped mouth was the only soft feature, almost feminine and somewhat incongruous in what was a very masculine face. Karen did not consider him handsome, but he was a man that any woman would automatically notice.

She suddenly realised that her appraisal was being returned. Her appearance did not seem to give him any more pleasure than his appearance had given her. To see her was to see the mirror-image of Kirsty, and to the man who had held Kirsty in his arms as she lay dying, that could only be disturbing. 'Your father said you wanted to see me,' she stated flatly, breaking the silence which had become very prickly.

'Yes. Thank you for coming. Please . . . take a seat. I want . . . to settle a few things with you.'

Her impression of strength had been so definite that it was another shock to realise that Hal's short speech had drained him. She stepped over to the chair near his bed and sat down. His throat worked convulsively for several moments before he spoke again, but the necessity for speech was in every strained muscle of his face.

'I don't understand. Kirsty always said she never wanted to have children. An abortion would have been more in keeping with her need to stay free. But having decided to have the child . . . why did she keep it a secret from me?'

Karen could hardly contain the contempt that burned on her tongue. It took every ounce of her control to speak coolly. 'No doubt an abortion would have been your solution.'

The grey eyes stabbed frustration at her. 'I would have welcomed a child and she knew it. Why didn't she tell me?'

Karen stared back at him, instinctively rejecting his assertions. 'It's easy for you to say that now, when Kirsty can't deny it. And easy to say you'd welcome a child when he's already a fact of life and you've seen him with your own eyes!'

A pained bewilderment shadowed his eyes, then it vanished, swept away by angry pride which settled into a hard, assessing look. 'She lied to me—no doubt she lied to you too. So what was the story, Karen?'

Karen bristled at the accusation. 'My sister did not lie to me!'

Hal studied her with hard, implacable eyes. 'Kirsty was pregnant when we came home from Jakarta, wasn't she? That was the . . . virus . . . that she picked up. The virus she couldn't shake off. The virus that prevented her from accompanying me to South America. My child!'

His voice wasn't hard. It shook with emotion, and again he swallowed convulsively before continuing. 'I didn't want to go without her. She said she'd follow when the doctor gave her a clean bill of health. And then . . . then she wrote that you were having a baby. You!' The word was a savage indictment of the lie. 'She said she had to stay with you, look after you until the baby was born. There were complications.'

His mouth curled in bitter derision. 'Quite a complication, wasn't it? So why did she give my child to you, Karen? And why did you take him?'

'Because . . .' Karen shook her head, absolutely stunned from the shock of Hal's attack—an attack which rocked her preconceptions of Hal's and Kirsty's relationship. Kirsty had never indicated that Hal was really concerned about her. She had never told Karen how she had explained her need for a leave of absence from the work she loved. The few things she had said had convinced Karen that Hal didn't care, wouldn't care. Had Kirsty lied to her? But for what purpose? It still didn't make sense.

'Because?' Hal prompted harshly.

Karen was too disturbed to monitor her answer. 'Because I wanted a child,' she murmured dazedly.

Again the pained bewilderment. 'Why didn't you have a child of your own? Why take mine?'

Tears of confusion swam into Karen's eyes. 'It was Kirsty's baby! Kirsty's!' she insisted defensively. 'And I didn't have one of my own because my husband couldn't. He was infertile.'

'My God!'

The appalled mutter was barely a croak but it snapped Karen's attention back to Hal. His face was twisted with pain and the grey eyes held all the bleakness of grieving torment. They turned to her with a look that seared her soul.

'That she should love you so much . . . and me so little . . .'

'It wasn't like that!' Karen burst out vehemently, unable to bear his reading of the situation. 'Kirsty didn't think you'd want to be tied down. She didn't want to be tied down herself. She wanted to share your life. The pregnancy wasn't planned. When it happened, she thought of me and Barry because we'd put our names down for an adoption and she preferred her child to come to us rather than go to anyone else.'

'Rather than to me—his natural father!' Hal bit out fiercely. His eyes shot bitter venom at her. 'You and your sister conspired to rob me of what was rightfully mine—my son.'

Before she knew it, Karen was on her feet, counter-attacking with all the venom she had felt since Kirsty had died. 'Rightfully yours!' she spat scornfully. 'By what right? Because one night you took my sister to bed with you and you didn't bother taking on the responsibility of contraception? Was it your body that carried a child for nine months and went through the labour pains of birth? By what possible right is he yours? No doubt your lust was satisfied that night and that was all you wanted.'

'She knew I would have wanted the child—she knew! And she kept him from me. You kept him.'

'And what would you have done, Hal?

Stayed home and looked after him or put the baby in a knapsack to trek around the world with you? Oh, Kirsty knew you all right. That's why she gave David to me.'

Beads of perspiration were breaking out on his forehead, but he gathered the strength for one more shot at her. 'You're wrong! And I'll get my son back from you if it's the last thing I do!'

Fear punched Karen's heart. Was she wrong? But why would Kirsty have deceived her about Hal? Karen wanted to scream at him, claw at him, but the saner part of her mind was appalled at what she had already done. Hal was strained to the limit. The heat of their exchange had obviously sent up his temperature; even his eyes looked feverish now. She had to remember how ill he really was. Fighting with him was the worst possible thing she could do anyway. It achieved nothing good either for him or her— or David.

She took a deep breath and forced her voice to a low, even tenor. 'Kidnapping is beyond the pale of the law, Hal, and the law is on my side. When you can stop thinking of yourself, perhaps you can start thinking of what's in David's best interests.'

'You too, Karen. He's been cheated of his father for three years,' Hal choked out bitterly. Again he swallowed several times. His eyes demanded her patience while hating his own weakness and hating her for being a witness to

it. 'How does a woman take a man's love ...
love, not lust ... before and after she bears him
a child, and keep his child a secret from him?
How can she do it?'

The pain was there now, clouding the hatred,
even though he was fighting to repress it. Karen
turned her gaze away, feeling sorry for him,
however twisted his point of view was. 'I don't
know,' she answered softly. 'I couldn't have
done what Kirsty did, but then I never was like
Kirsty. We only look the same. I didn't
understand her relationship with you; it always
seemed wrong to me. She said she didn't want
to lose you—that's all I know.'

'She didn't want anything to change,' Hal
corrected harshly.

'Or was it you who didn't want anything to
change?' countered Karen, stung to a further
defence of her sister. 'You could have asked
Kirsty to marry you. God knows you ...
enjoyed ... her companionship long enough!'

A savage mockery stabbed from steel-grey
eyes. 'Didn't you know anything about your
sister? Kirsty wouldn't have married anyone.
Not anyone! As for me, it's plain now that she
regarded me as a convenience.'

Karen paled. It wasn't true! Kirsty had loved
him, she knew that for certain. Kirsty wouldn't
have told him about David unless she had loved
him. Karen's mind whirled with sickening
thoughts. Kirsty had always wanted to be free.
But to give up her baby when she needn't have

. . . it was incomprehensible to Karen. And if Hal had been cheated, what was she to do?

She stared at him in guilty concern. His eyes were closed and his hands were clenched into fists as if he was willing his body to give him the strength he wanted. His breathing was harsh and laboured.

'I'm sorry,' she muttered, not quite knowing what she was apologising for. 'This can't be doing you any good. I think I'd better go.'

The eyelids snapped open and determined purpose glittered at her. 'You haven't seen the last of me, Karen. No matter where you go, I'll come after you.'

There was no point in saying goodbye. Karen walked out of his room, all too aware that she would see Hal again. And the future looked more frightening than it had ever done.

CHAPTER FOUR

HE was home.

Ever since the night she had visited Hal in hospital Karen had been suffering varying degrees of mental and emotional anguish. The justice or injustice of her position as David's single parent was a dilemma she could not resolve. And now Hal had come after her. He had arrived in Sydney this morning.

It had been in the afternoon newspapers. Owen had told Karen it would be this week, so it wasn't as if she hadn't been prepared. She had had two months to get herself prepared for Hal's homecoming, but the photograph in the newspaper had badly jolted her. The hard, unsmiling face had seemed to look straight at her with accusing eyes.

Those eyes were still haunting her, hours later. She had carried out her normal routine as if nothing abnormal was going on, but the knowledge of Hal's presence in Sydney was a heavy weight on her heart. With David safely tucked in bed for the night she could relax the tight control she had held on her emotions.

She wanted to cry, but she knew that would serve no purpose. The newspaper article had mentioned that Hal would be interviewed on television tonight and it was almost time for the current affairs programme which was to feature the interview. She had to watch it. There might be something . . . words, expressions, a mental attitude . . . some indication of his intentions.

She returned to the family room, switched on the television and set the control to the channel owned by Owen Chissolm. She made herself a cup of coffee and propped herself on the kitchen stool to await Hal's appearance.

The programme began with a recapitulation of his career as a television reporter and producer/director of news documentaries. The highlight was inevitably the terrorist bomb attack which had taken the life of Kirsty Balfour, Hal's closest associate. The reminder was painful, but Karen steeled herself to block out the pain. It was Hal who was all-important now.

Her whole body tensed as he strode on to the set, his tall, lithe frame emitting a fitness which Karen knew to be false: Owen had told her it would be at least another month before Hal's convalescence was complete. But his face was tanned, he moved with apparent ease, and the blue and grey sweater and grey slacks emphasised the attractiveness of his dark good looks.

He was heartily welcomed by the host of the show, who barely gave him time to sit before plunging into chat. 'You must be glad to be home after such a traumatic experience, Hal.'

'Yes. I came as soon as the doctors cleared me for travel. I'm afraid I wasn't a very patient patient,' he added sardonically.

'You look well enough—particularly after such a serious operation. One of the pieces of metal the doctors removed was lodged next to your heart, wasn't it?'

'Yes. The surgeons had to cut through part of one lung to get to it. Fortunately I have a very strong constitution. I believe they didn't give me much chance of survival at one stage, but I certainly had no intention of dying.' A grim smile curled his lips. 'Life was suddenly very necessary to me.'

Karen's heart lurched. Because of David. And he had come home as soon as he could for David.

'I understand you're now retiring from the active field and taking up administration. Was it your brush with death which motivated this decision?'

'No. But it gave me an awareness of family responsibilities. I shall remain based in Sydney from now on . . .'

Well, there could be nothing more definite than that, Karen thought miserably.

'. . . My father keeps telling me he's not as young as he used to be,' Hal added drily.

The interviewer chuckled. 'Are you telling us that Owen Chissolm is thinking of retiring?'

Hal gave a short, mocking laugh. 'Never! But he's always been keen for me to take a greater interest in home affairs, and I'm now more inclined to agree with him.'

They talked on about the Chissolm media empire, but Karen had heard all she needed to know. Hal was home to stay, and she had no doubt that his 'family responsibilities' referred to David. She was very much afraid that Hal would not be content to be a Sunday father, but she could not give David up to him. He was her son too. Surely the years and the love she had given to David counted as much as Hal's rights as a natural father?

She had been forced to concede that Hal did have rights. His assertions in the hospital had been reinforced by what Owen had told her last Sunday. Owen had always been fair to her and she trusted him. When she had broached the subject of Kirsty's relationship with Hal, she was sure that Owen had given her the truth as he knew it. Every word he had spoken was carved into her memory.

'Some four years ago Hal came to me and discussed the various options he could take up should he give the travelling up. I was delighted. I assumed at the time that he intended marrying Kirsty, but nothing came of it. And he changed. It's difficult to explain, not something you can really put your finger on. There was more of a compulsion to go to dangerous places, a recklessness which I didn't think was natural to him. It was more fitting to a youth, and Hal was past that. He wouldn't

talk to me about it. I once made a critical
comment on his relationship with Kirsty and he
told me to mind my own damned business. He
became . . . unreachable to me. I blamed Kirsty
for it.'

And she had blamed Hal—wrongly, blindly
and perhaps unjustly. Karen knew now that her
sister's dying words had been a wish to make
restoration for what she had taken from him.
Karen also knew that she was being forced to
pay the price of her sister's debt, yet what
would be the final cost to herself? And David?
A child was not a parcel one could just pass
around, and she loved him with a fiercely
protective mother-love. All she could really do
was hope Hal would be reasonable, but judging
from his hard manner tonight, Karen could not
dredge up much faith in that hope.

The telephone rang. She stared at it, tension
screaming along her nerves. Was it Hal? The
current affairs programme had ended while she
had been brooding over her dilemma. Gingerly
she picked the receiver up. Her mouth was
completely dry, and she quickly worked some
saliva into it.

'Karen Aylward,' she croaked.

'It's Barry, Karen.'

Shock rippled through her. Barry! She had
neither seen nor heard from him in the two
years since their divorce. She heard him take a
deep breath.

'I was just watching a programme on

television and heard about Kirsty. I was out of the country and didn't hear the news when it happened, Karen. I know how very close you two were. It must have been . . .' another deep breath, 'you must feel terribly alone. If there's anything I can do, help in some way . . .'

Tears swam into her eyes, grief welling again at the reminder of her loneliness. And with Hal threatening the fabric she had made of her life, she felt more alone than ever. 'That's . . . that's kind of you, Barry,' she choked out. 'Thank you, but there's nothing you can do.' Not about Kirsty, or about David. Barry hadn't wanted David.

A long sigh whispered over the line. 'I guess Kirsty's boy is a comfort to you.'

A comfort and an agonising worry, but Karen swallowed down her private pain. 'Yes, he is. He's a wonderful little boy.'

Another sigh. 'I know I let you down badly over him. I'm sorry, Karen. I was just one hell of a mess at the time—no good to myself, let alone to you or anyone else.'

'It's past, Barry,' Karen said quickly, not feeling up to re-hashing those memories.

'Yes, it is past. That's what I wanted to say. It's been a long time, but I still care for you, Karen, very much. I want to see you again. There's something very important that I want to tell you. Can we meet?'

Her mind whirled. Did she want to see Barry again and risk re-opening feelings she had put behind her? David was her life now, and Barry had rejected David.

'Is there someone else, Karen?'

'No, it's not that,' she blurted out, yet there was someone else. There was Hal ... Hal coming to take David away from her if he could. It was difficult to think of anything else, let alone some kind of reunion with Barry.

'Karen, please ... I must see you. We missed out on so much together. I know it was mainly my fault, but we did share a lot of things and now it's possible for us to share a great deal more. I promise you it's very important.'

Years of sharing, good and bad, the appeal touched Karen's heart. She could not dismiss it. She would feel too mean, unforgiving. 'All right, Barry. When do you want to meet?'

'Tomorrow night?' he suggested eagerly.

And if Hal came or called? No, that would be impossibly awkward. Hal knew that Barry had rejected David and it would look highly questionable if he found her with her ex-husband. David was her first concern. And obviously Hal's, so surely he would have contacted her by the weekend. But caution was certainly wise.

'That doesn't suit me, Barry,' she said firmly. 'How about next Monday night? You could come to dinner.'

'That's great, Karen. What time do you want me?'

The relief and pleasure in his voice took the

edge off the strain she felt. He sounded like the old Barry, the man she had married. A smile warmed her own voice. 'Seven-thirty will be fine.'

'Thanks, Karen—thanks a million! I'll see you then.'

He rang off, and Karen slowly put the telephone down, conscious of far too many burdens on her heart. What she owed Kirsty ... what she owed Hal ... what she owed Barry. Surely there was a limit to the giving, a point where it turned around and she was the beneficiary? It was probably a mistake to see Barry again, but she could not have refused him. She hoped something would be settled with Hal by Monday night.

For the next two days it was extremely difficult for Karen to hide her inner tension from David and act naturally with him. The impulse to hug him close on any pretext was almost impossible to quell. The sense of time running out was overwhelming.

Hal didn't call; he came. It was only the third night after he had arrived back in Sydney. The doorbell rang at precisely eight o'clock, and Karen knew intuitively whose hand was applying the pressure. In some ways it was a relief that the feared confrontation had come, yet her heart felt like a lump of lead as she went to open the door.

The grey eyes which appraised her held no shade of softness, no grain of sympathy. They were a bleak sea of cold reserve. They chilled Karen even while her instincts were picking up other vibrations. The sheer physical impact of the man was much greater than she had anticipated. The strength emanating from him in a hospital bed was a weak reflection of the aura of ruthless purpose he carried now. Fear gave birth to a bristling antagonism. She would not let this man take everything she held dear away from her.

Her own eyes hardened as she broke the prickly silence. 'Would you like to come in?'

'Thank you,' he answered curtly.

'I'm afraid David is asleep,' she stated with a certain amount of hostile satisfaction as Hal stepped inside.

'I expected him to be by this time. But I would like to see him before we talk.' It was more a demand than a request.

Karen knew she would win no points by objecting. 'Follow me,' she invited coolly, and led the way to David's room. She switched on the bedside lamp which spread a dim glow over the sleeping child, and stepped aside.

Hal gazed down at his son with no perceptible softening on his face, yet there seemed to be a yearning tenderness in the light brush of fingertips across David's fine-skinned cheek. Then his gaze lifted and swept around the room, taking in the child-fantasy pictures on the walls, the aeroplane print curtains, the shelves which held David's story-books and little ornaments, the mobile of plastic animals hanging above the bed and the transfers of fairy-tale characters on the cupboard doors. He stared at Karen for a long moment before looking down at his son once more. It was he who switched off the lamp. He moved briskly from the room and waited in the hallway as Karen quietly closed the door behind them.

Her heart was thudding painfully. Had David's room impressed him? What judgement had Hal made of her in there? His thoughts were an enigma, too well hidden by the hard, impassive mask which kept her firmly at a distance. Without a word but with a churning mind, Karen led him into the living room.

'Please sit down. Would you like a drink? Coffee?'

'No, thank you.' His gaze dropped to her hand which was nervously fingering her crumpled skirt. 'But if you'd like one . . .'

'No, I just thought . . .' She made a vaguely dismissive gesture and concentrated hard on pulling herself together as she took the nearest armchair.

Hal lowered his elegant length into the opposite chair. He was dressed in semi-formal attire tonight, finely tailored slacks, a tweed sports coat, silk shirt and tie. Karen was very conscious of the fact that she was in the same clothes she had worn all day at the pre-school kindergarten where she worked. The green sweater still had a spot of paint on it and the tan skirt was badly creased. She hadn't even tidied her long hair since this morning and the lipstick she had worn was surely eaten off by now. She felt at a distinct disadvantage, but it was too late to do anything about her appearance.

'You're not surprised to see me,' he stated flatly.

'You said you'd come,' she replied just as flatly.

'I want David, Karen.'

Her stomach knotted at the calm, relentless declaration and as he spoke on, each word was a hammer-blow to her heart.

'I am his father. I've been consulting with lawyers for the last two days. I'm going to get my son, one way or another.'

Karen could feel the blood draining from her face, but she summoned every bit of will-power to control the weakness she felt. She didn't want to fight Hal. It would do none of them any good, particularly David. She had to convince him that a more reasonable course would be best for all of them. 'Don't do it, Hal. You can't win. I'm the only parent he's ever known. I'm sorry that you were deceived in the way you were, but you can't honestly believe that two wrongs can make a right? Any kind of conflict between us has to be harmful for David.'

'He's only three, young enough to adjust—so the psychiatrists tell me.'

'And do they say it's good to deprive him of his mother?' Karen fired at him, angered beyond control by his callousness.

Hal threw the shot back at her with unerring aim. 'You were only too happy to deprive him of his father!'

For a moment the room seemed to throb with their mutual antagonism. Karen shook her head despairingly. 'He's always been my child. I love him. He loves me. Can't you see that?'

It did not move him one iota. 'Karen, if you want a child of your own, there's nothing to stop you. You're divorced. Take any man you like. As Kirsty took me,' he added bitterly.

The cruelty of the jibe brought tears to her eyes. 'There's no one I like. There hasn't been anyone since my husband. David is all I have.'

Something flickered in his eyes, something indefinably dangerous. 'Is that so?' he asked in a deceptively soft voice.

He hadn't softened. Karen sensed a change in him, but he hadn't softened. It was none of his business whether she had been with any man or not, unless he was looking for facts to hold against her in a custody case. 'My whole life has revolved around David since Kirsty gave him to me,' she declared pointedly.

He made no comment. The grey eyes seemed to be making a reappraisal of her, but it was a hard reappraisal and oddly discomfiting. She worked on smoothing out the sharpness from her voice. Fighting Hal could only embitter him further against her. She had to break this impasse they had reached.

'Please ... can't we try to work something out? I want to be fair to you. Can't you be fair to me?'

Her plea fell on stony ground. 'What do you call fair, Karen? I understand that you and David have been spending the occasional Sunday with my father over the last few weeks. Do you think an occasional Sunday is enough for me too?'

'No.' Her eyes begged for some hint of giving but there was none. 'I thought every Sunday to begin with. Until David got used to you. Then ...' She sucked in a steadying breath and plunged on, hoping he would agree to her terms. 'Then every other Saturday as well as Sundays. You'll be busy working during the week anyway, and I ... I'd like one free day with David every fortnight. Is that unreasonable?'

He was surprised. There was only the minutest change in his expression but the savage glitter of mockery was gone from his eyes. 'That is ... a more generous offer ... than I anticipated from you.'

'Generous! It'll be like cutting half my life away. Can you even begin to appreciate that?' Tears blurred her eyes again and she hastily looked down, hoping he had not seen them. She couldn't be weak now. She had to be strong. As strong as he was. But dear God! One Saturday a fortnight. What was she going to do with herself over the long weekends that David was away?

'Since you have no other attachment in your life, perhaps you'll consider a different proposition.'

Karen glanced up warily. The grey eyes were boring into her, ruthless in their intent.

'I don't want a custody case any more than you do—I don't care for such a private affair to be dragged in front of the public eye. But I want David. Not on any part-time basis, Karen. I want him as you've had him for the last three years.'

He paused, then delivered the punchline with devastating directness. 'You can either fight me . . . or you can marry me. And in David's best interests, I think you should marry me.'

CHAPTER FIVE

'You're mad!' Karen whispered, appalled at the very thought of marriage to her sister's lover.

'Not at all. It was you who pointed out to me that if I wanted to be the father of the child, I should marry the mother.' His mouth curled to one side. 'And if you remember, the injuries I sustained were not to the head, Karen. They were closer to the heart.'

She recalled the odd way he had looked at her earlier . . . the hard, glittering appraisal. Had he been thinking then that she could take Kirsty's place? That she could fill the role that Kirsty had refused, wife and mother? Or was he intent on revenge? Karen shivered with revulsion.

'I'm not Kirsty. I can't take her place, Hal. Please, can't we . . .'

He gave a mirthless laugh. 'I wouldn't want you to take Kirsty's place, Karen. You couldn't. I simply want to be a father to my son.' A gleam of mockery lightened his eyes. 'You should be grateful that I'm giving you any choice at all.'

Grateful! He really was mad! He was acting as if he had the whip hand and it was she who had all the legal guns. She felt like spitting that out at him, but open hostility had to be avoided. If they both moved into entrenched positions it was David who would be caught in the crossfire. She drew in a steadying breath and spoke with the calm control of absolute confidence.

'I've bent over backwards to be fair to you, Hal, offering more access to David than any court would grant you. You can't take David away from me. I've had legal advice too. There's no way a court will set aside those adoption papers, not even if you can prove that you were deceived. If you can't be reasonable . . .'

He smiled, but there was no good humour in it. 'Then you received bad advice, Karen. It's not a question of whether or not Kirsty deceived me. The fact is that the adoption papers themselves were fraudulently prepared, and a court will be only too willing to set them aside when that fraud is exposed.'

It shook her—but maybe that was his purpose. 'Those papers are perfectly legal. I've had them checked.'

One eyebrow rose mockingly. 'Have your solicitor take another look at them, Karen. With particular attention to the entry under FATHER OF THE CHILD. It says "unknown". Kirsty had to write that so she could have the baby adopted without my knowledge. But the father of the child *was* known, Karen. Even if you are prepared to perjure yourself by swearing that you didn't know the father's identity, your case will still be blown to bits. Apart from the medical evidence, I have an unimpeachable witness who will tell the truth—your ex-husband.'

Barry? Barry would testify against her? Was that the important thing he had to tell her? But Hal had only come home that day of Barry's telephone call. Her mind was reeling with shock. If what Hal said was true, that the adoption papers were fraudulent . . . and it had to be true or he would not be so arrogantly confident . . . then she was in deep trouble. She might lose David. But why would Barry give such damning evidence without talking to her about it? Was Hal bluffing?

'I take it you've spoken to Barry,' she clipped out, hiding her terrifying uncertainties.

'Not personally, no. But my lawyers have obtained a signed statement from him. They're very thorough.'

He was enjoying his triumph, enjoying each turn of the screw. Karen hated him with a more virulent hatred than she had ever thought herself capable of. All her heartburn over being fair to him was bitter ashes in her mouth. 'You've just been leading me on, haven't you? Ever since you got here.'

'It was interesting to see just how far you'd go.'

She shook her head . . . stupid, gullible fool that she had been, trying to do the right thing.

Her eyes blasted him with the depth of her contempt. 'You're nothing but a black-hearted bastard!'

'Then I'm living up to the image you've held of me for years, aren't I?' Hal retorted with bite, then relaxed into a silkier tone. 'Come now, Karen, I'm being very reasonable. I appreciate that you love David and don't want to lose him. It's really very simple. To keep him, all you have to do is marry me.'

'I can't marry you!' she flared, goaded beyond thought by his taunting manner.

His mouth tightened into a hard, implacable line. 'Then we have nothing left to talk about.' He stood up and the grey eyes were glacial. 'I'll have my lawyers start proceedings tomorrow. I regret that you don't have the strength of your convictions, but since you find the idea of marriage to me more distasteful than a life without David, I'll see you in court, Karen.'

Having thrown down the gauntlet he turned to go. Fear gripped Karen's heart and panic churned through her mind. If he won custody ... he would employ the best lawyers ... she didn't have the money to fight him ... if she lost David ...

'Wait!'

Her urgent cry stopped him. Slowly he swung around and despite his leanness, he looked even more formidable than his father had done that first morning. Karen rose to her feet, impelled to stand up to him yet knowing she could not match his power. But marriage was equally impossible.

'Well?' he prompted.

'I need time . . . time to think about it,' she blurted out.

'Certainly. I'll bend over backwards to be fair. It might make the choice a little clearer for you if you get some more accurate legal advice. I'll give you until this time next week to make up your mind. But on one condition . . .'

He paused, and the savage glitter in his eyes struck more fear into Karen's heart. 'And what's that?' she asked, a sickening turmoil of emotion furring her voice.

Hal smiled and leaned indolently against the door-jamb, his arms folded as if all the time in the world was on his side. 'You and David are to spend the weekend with me at my father's house, so that we can all get to know one another better.'

Karen didn't think she could stand two days with him let alone a lifetime of marriage. She found herself wringing her hands and instantly stopped the revealing action, but she could not stop the wringing of her heart. 'Why are you doing this to me?' she asked in helpless despair.

Again that curl of the lip which was not really a smile. His eyes were cold, hard steel. 'Because I intend to have the mother of my child as my wife.'

Her stomach heaved with nausea. 'It's not me you want. It's because I look like Kirsty, isn't it? Well, I'm not Kirsty, Hal.'

He was completely unperturbed by her vehement denial. 'I'm well aware of that. Kirsty died in my arms, remember? It's you I want, Karen.'

'You're a monster,' Karen whispered.

'Yes—a monster without any natural feelings at all. Isn't that right, Karen?'

So he was taking his vengeance for what she had said to him in the hospital . . . words spoken out of grief . . . words she had believed to be true. And now she was reaping the bitterness that had been sown with a mistake . . . an honest mistake. She lifted her hands in a gesture of helplessness. 'It's an impossible situation.'

'Not at all. It's quite clear-cut.'

She stared at him, looking desperately for one chink in his armour, but it was impervious. 'I've always hated you,' she said in hopeless appeal.

'Your last marriage was presumably based on love, but it didn't work. Perhaps hate is a better basis for starting with—things can't get worse, they can only improve.'

His cynicism was a sour indictment of any form of love. 'You can't want to . . .' Karen bit the words back, wary now of even mentioning the word love to Hal. 'What kind of marriage did you have in mind?'

'The normal kind.'

He pushed away from the door-jamb and

strolled back towards her. Each lazy step seemed to carry a physical threat to Karen. She wanted to turn and run away from him, but there was no running away from this situation. She stood her ground, but everything inside her cringed from his nearness as he came to a halt a mere pace from her.

'You've always wanted children, haven't you? So desperately that you took my child. And it would be good for David to have brothers and sisters, don't you think? I never do anything by halves, Karen. I work on the principle of all or nothing. I may have been fooled by Kirsty, but I won't let myself be cheated again. All or nothing,' Hal repeated softly, but the words carried relentless purpose.

She couldn't go to bed with him. She just couldn't, Karen thought wildly. Not even for David's sake. She would never be able to forget that Kirsty had been there before her. She stared up at the hard grey eyes and felt absolute despair. 'It can't work. Apart from hating each other we have nothing in common.'

He gave a mirthless laugh. 'My dear Karen, it's not hatred but love that will bind us together. We both love David; we have that in common. We both loved Kirsty; we have that in common. And we both face a life of personal loneliness, fighting over the love of a child. And that, too, we have in common.'

He made a very deliberate point of looking at his watch. 'I'll give you five minutes to make up your mind about the weekend.'

As much as she recoiled from the idea, Karen knew that she had to keep her options open. And Owen would be there. Surely Owen's presence would ensure that the weekend was passed in a reasonably civilised manner. And it gave her more time; that was the important thing. Time to see Barry on Monday night, before she had to make an irrevocable decision.

'I'll come.'

'Good!' For a moment there was a glint of satisfaction in his eyes, but it winked out as Hal continued speaking. 'One more thing, Karen. If any of the advice you received was any good, you'll know that David has the right to know his natural parents. Before I pick you up tomorrow night, I insist that you tell him I'm his father.'

'To-morrow night?'

'It's Friday tomorrow,' he reminded her drily. 'The weekend is usually regarded as starting after work on Friday. I'll be here for you and David at six o'clock. You'll be dining with my father and myself after we put David to bed.'

So little time to get her thoughts and feelings into order! And to prepare David!

'You can tell David I had to go away and was caught up in wars overseas, but now I'm back home and I'm back for good.' Hal's eyes carried a savage indictment as he added, 'No need to tell him that his very existence was kept hidden from me.'

Her cheeks burnt with guilty shame. But it hadn't been all her fault. Couldn't he see that? She tried to reach past his bitterness. 'I'm sorry, Hal, but I had no reason not to believe what Kirsty told me.'

'And a very good reason to believe her,' he mocked.

Karen dropped her gaze, weary from battling the pressure he was exerting on her mind and emotions. She saw his hand lift and flinched away from its touch as he attempted to tilt her chin. Her eyes flashed up to Hal's, sharp with the fear of his forcefulness.

He was about to speak when his face suddenly went rigid. His gaze seemed fastened on the base of her throat. The hand he had lifted reached forward and pulled at the fine gold chain which Karen always wore, the exact match of the fine gold chain that Kirsty had worn. Every nerve in Karen's body tensed in protest, yet she could not move. Hal stared down at the little jade koala for a long time, and somehow Karen was mesmerised by his absorption in it. A muscle flinched along his jawline. When he finally looked up, his eyes held a wild, dangerous glitter.

'Well, a koala is easier to catch than a bird, isn't it?'

Her heart leapt as he moved closer. No-o-o . . . the word quivered through her mind as his hands moved around her back, gathering her into an embrace. She meant to say it out loud. She told herself to say it out loud. But somehow it got strangled in her throat as one of his hands slid up under her hair and caressed the back of her neck.

No-o-o ... the whisper of breath expelled from her trembling lips did not carry the sound. His mouth came closer and closer. Couldn't he see the torment of protest in her eyes? She was not Kirsty. She was not!

But his mouth took hers with compelling hunger, and his body was pressing against hers, igniting a thousand pinpricks of awareness, awakening sexual sensations that had lain dormant for years. It had been so long since she had been held like this, kissed like this, and the turmoil of emotion that Hal had stirred tonight, begged for some release. She almost gave in to the insidious sensuality of his kiss, but she could not forget who he was.

Horror at her own vulnerability drove her hands against his shoulders. She jerked her head back and pushed some distance between them, her eyes wildly accusing him of unspeakable things. 'I'm not Kirsty!' she gasped. Her chest was heaving as if she had run a long race.

He smiled, while his fingers stroked a featherlight caress down her flushed cheek. 'No. You're surprisingly different, Karen. I was merely starting off the getting-to-know-you process.'

All the frustration, anguish and rage which had been piling up in her demanded some outlet. 'You're the most despicable, revolting apology for a human being it's ever been my misfortune to meet, Hal Chissolm!'

'Splendid! I'm glad you feel that way. Taming you will now give me so much more satisfaction. If you decide to marry me.'

Never! The word shrieked around her mind, but she held it in with grim control. He enjoyed provoking her. He relished this cat and mouse game. Be damned if she would give him any more satisfaction than she had to! Let him flick the whip as much as he liked and she would show no reaction. That was the way to deal with him while she paid for the time she needed. She wrapped herself in icy dignity.

'I want you to go now,' she said coldly.

'Of course. You have some packing to do for the weekend.'

Hal let her go and she strode quickly for the door, needing to hurry him on his way. He followed her without another word until Karen held the front door open for him. Then he paused beside her, forcing her to lift her gaze to his. Her body screamed with tension but the grey eyes were flint-hard.

'Don't fool yourself, Karen. I hold all the cards. Six o'clock tomorrow. And be very careful with David. Much less traumatic if he can love the father who loves him. We do want what's in David's best interests, don't we?'

'Yes,' she bit out, fiercely resenting the power he was wielding.

Hal gave her cheek a derisive pat of approval, then at last he was striding away from her.

Karen watched him go with sick, helpless eyes. Owen Chissolm's Rolls Royce stood at the kerb. The chauffeur alighted and held a door open for Hal. Wealth and power, she thought despairingly as the car drove off. She wondered what Owen thought of Hal's plans and then brushed the thought aside. Owen would not interfere; he had his son back home where he wanted him.

The car disappeared around a corner, and Karen stood alone with the darkness of the night. Her gaze lifted to a star-studded sky. The pinpricks of light were so far away, unreachable. Her mind sent out a despairing message . . . why, Kirsty? Why did you do it? To him and to me?

There was no answer.

CHAPTER SIX

IT WAS impossible for David to contain his excitement. No sooner had they arrived at the pre-school kindergarten centre than he was boasting to all and sundry that his father was coming home. This very night! And he and Mummy were going to stay with his father for the whole weekend.

Karen was faced with some very awkward and embarrassing questions. The women on the staff knew that she was divorced and their curiosity was aroused. A reconciliation was the common assumption. Which reminded Karen how urgently she needed to see Barry. Monday night could not come soon enough for her, not because she had a reconciliation in mind, but she needed her legal position with David clarified as soon as possible.

She had never told anyone that David was her adopted son and the relationships involving Kirsty, Hal and herself were far too complex and far too personal to be bandied about in a staff room. She fobbed off the questions by saying that David's father had been overseas for some years and they were having the weekend together to work out what was best for David's future. Her request for a leave of absence on Monday was granted with an understanding smile.

Karen was still grimacing with the irony of that very mistaken understanding as she slipped out to the public telephone box on the nearby street-corner to make the call to her solicitor. Far from wanting to be with David's father, she needed the time to find out if she had any chance of fighting him and winning. In as calm a voice as she could manage, she related Hal's claims to her solicitor, asked him to double-check her legal position, and made an appointment to see him on Monday. The concern he expressed over the new complication did nothing to ease Karen's mind.

The fear that had been churning through her since last night took a deeper turn. If Hal's lawyers could get the adoption papers set aside then she would have to fight a straight custody case—or marry Hal Chissolm. And how could she bring herself to do that when everything inside her recoiled from the idea? But the thought of losing David was even worse.

For the rest of the day Karen seethed with resentment at the choice Hal was forcing on her. It was very difficult to bear David's fever of happy anticipation as she dressed him ready for his father's arrival. She sourly wondered if Hal would live up to his son's expectation. At least he could not criticise her part in imparting the news of his father to David. The look on David's face as he took up a watch at his

bedroom window proved that she had done Hal
justice.

Which was more than Hal could say for his
treatment of her, Karen thought angrily as she
hurried to dress herself. Pride dictated that her
appearance could not be faulted either. She
needed every possible bolster to self-confidence
in a situation which she sensed was beyond her
ability to control. In her nervous haste she
automatically chose her best dress, then with a
shudder of distaste, realised that it was also
green, Kirsty's favourite colour. The last thing
she wanted to do was remind Hal of Kirsty. Not
that she could do much to prevent it, she
thought despairingly.

When she was finally ready she eyed her
reflection in the mirror with a grim satisfaction.
Her hair, freshly washed and blow-dried,
curved around her shoulders in a neat, tidy fall,
its deep chestnut colour gleaming richly. A
touch of green eye-shadow and a subtle eye-
liner highlighted her large hazel eyes. Her
mouth was perfectly lipsticked. The fine wool
of the corn-yellow dress hugged her slim figure,
giving a soft emphasis to her very feminine
curves. She could not help looking like Kirsty,
but in her own way she looked as good as she
could.

'He's here!'

David's shriek of excitement set her nerves
jangling. He came pelting into her bedroom, his
little face alight with joyous anticipation.

'He came in Pop's car. Can I go and meet him, Mummy? Can I?'

'May I,' she corrected automatically, 'and yes, you may.'

He was off like a rocket. Karen quickly zipped her suitcase shut and carried it out to the entrance hallway where David's bag was already placed. The front door was wide open. David's headlong rush down the front path suddenly faltered to a stop as he took in the tall man who was unlatching the gate.

Hal smiled and Karen's heart gave a queasy lurch. His striking good looks were immeasurably enhanced by that warmly welcoming smile. She found herself wishing he would smile at her like that.

'Daddy?' David's piping voice held a breathless quaver of uncertainty.

Hal swung the gate open and crouched down to his son's level, his arms outstretched in invitation. 'Yes, David, I'm your daddy, and I'm very, very happy to be with you at last.'

David walked forward shyly, then in a last little rush he flung his arms around Hal's neck. In one fluid action Hal was lifting him, hugging him possessively, claiming his son, loving him.

Karen fought to hold back tears. She had tried to be everything to David, giving him all the love and attention she could, but today he had shown all too clearly how much he wanted a father. And Hal's face was lit with the same happiness that beamed from David's. However hard and bitter he was towards her, it was obvious that his heart was more than open to his son.

He was not the monster she had called him last night. Not to David. Yet even as her mind acknowledged these facts, the acute pain of loss in her heart was excruciating. It was bad enough to see David's love being directed on to Hal; the thought of losing him entirely was unbearable.

It took all Karen's will-power to hide her pain from David as Hal carried him back to her, laughingly answering the questions that David's lively curiosity was firing at him. Owen Chissolm's chauffeur followed them, and Hal waved him forward to collect the suitcases from the hallway. Karen thanked the chauffeur and locked the door after him. Only then did she meet the grey eyes which had chilled her last night. The smile was still on Hal's face, but there was more than happiness in his eyes. There was triumph.

'Daddy said we have to collect you, Mummy,' David crowed at her, and the triumph in Hal's eyes seemed to be reflected in his.

Hal shifted his support of David to one arm and before Karen could evade his intention, he curved his other arm around her shoulders. 'You mustn't hold back, Karen. David and I want you with us, don't we, son?'

He gurgled agreement, and her body was stiff with protest. Hal assumed too much. Yet his touch made her heart catapult around her chest.

'Relax. We're all together now,' said Hal with suggestive warmth as he walked her towards the car.

But she couldn't relax. She was swamped with an awareness of the body brushing against hers, the lean, muscular length of it, the strong masculinity which reminded her all too sharply that she was a woman; a woman who had not been touched by a man for a long time.

It was an enormous relief to her when Hal handed her into the back passenger seat. It was even more of a relief when David was placed between them for the drive to the Chissolm home. But while there was a slight physical separation from Hal during the trip to the Chissolm mansion in Turramurra, there was no emotional one. If David was not including 'Mummy' in the conversation, Hal did, and all the time Hal's eyes seemed to be reminding her that this was what she could share if she made the choice to marry him.

With a sinking heart Karen realised she had made a terrible mistake in making this weekend bargain with Hal. She had thought to buy some necessary time, but Hal was using the time to far better advantage, forming an emotional tie between himself and David. She could not doubt that the love he was showering on David was anything but genuine, and David was basking in it. If she did not marry Hal, and he forced her to a custody case, David was going to be hurt whichever way it was decided.

The driveway up to Owen's home depressed her even further. The huge brick edifice was set in beautifully landscaped grounds which featured a tennis court and a swimming-pool as well as magnificent gardens. Hal could give David everything in a material sense, far more than Karen could ever afford. Under the altered legal circumstances a judge would have to take that into consideration.

The front door was opened by the butler before they had even alighted from the car. Karen had noticed on her previous visits with Owen that the house-staff seemed trained to cater for every need with smooth efficiency. Karen clung on to David's hand, hoping to keep him as a buffer between herself and another embrace from Hal.

'Why don't you run ahead and say hello to Pop, David,' Hal suggested brightly. 'Your mother and I will be right behind you.'

The little boy was off in an instant, all too eager to tell Pop about Daddy, and leaving Karen at the mercy of the man who held all the cards. And who was playing them with daunting skill. She glanced up at him apprehensively, wondering what this move signified. To her surprise his expression was warm with appreciation.

'I wanted to thank you for the good job you

did with David. It meant more to me than I can say.'

A little rush of hope voiced her reply. 'I'm trying to be fair, Hal. Won't you consider a compromise?'

Instantly his face hardened. 'No. I want David or both of you. I'll take no less than that.'

'But why? You can't really want me, and David won't be happy if you . . .'

The savage look in his eyes silenced her even before he spoke, and the words cut straight to her soul. 'I sacrificed myself for your sister and my reward . . . my reward, Karen . . . was that she gave my child to you. To keep my child you're going to have to sacrifice yourself to me. I call that fair. Don't you?'

He took her elbow and steered her up the front steps while Karen was too dazed to protest. What did he mean . . . he had sacrificed himself for Kirsty? It made no sense, and Hal gave her no time to question. He ushered her into an elegant sitting room where Owen was indulgently listening to David's news.

'And here's your daddy now,' he declared, almost pushing his grandson back to Hal as he came forward to greet Karen. His whole bearing bespoke a deep pleasure as he took Karen's hands. 'How lovely you look tonight! I'm delighted that you accepted Hal's invitation, Karen. I want you to have a happy weekend with us, and if there's anything I can do to make your stay . . .'

'I think that's my line, Dad,' Hal cut in sardonically.

Owen glanced sharply at him. Despite the slight curve of Hal's mouth there was a cold reserve in the gaze that met his father's. It was instantly apparent that although Hal had come home, there was no close understanding between father and son. Karen remembered Owen's words that Hal had become unreachable to him and the breach had obviously not been mended.

Owen's smile to her was a smooth withdrawal from his son's declared territory. 'I want you to know that you're always welcome here, Karen,' he finished warmly.

Karen forced herself to answer. 'Thank you, Owen.' The words trembled from her lips, but she was too shaken to say more. There could be no help from Owen, no point in even discussing the situation with him. Without a doubt Hal held the whip hand. Whatever Owen privately thought of his son's plans, if indeed he knew them at all, he would not do anything which would alienate Hal further. He loved his son. And Karen was totally alone.

'If you'll excuse us, Dad, I'll take Karen and David upstairs and show them their rooms.'

'Of course.'

Owen released her hands as Hal took her arm, and Karen caught a look of troubled concern in the old man's eyes before Hal turned her away. Owen liked her, she knew he did. But all she could expect from him was sympathy.

Karen was even more shaken when Hal led them into David's room. The furniture was all new, painted a bright canary yellow with a white trim. Cupboards, drawers, shelves and desk were all fitted into a classy unit which stretched around two walls. Matching curtains and bedspread featured Australian flora and fauna. A huge bean-bag in the shape of David's favourite television character, Humphrey B. Bear, squatted on the floor near the bed. All the toys to delight a three-year-old were stacked around the room, and even a set of felt pens with colouring-in books were waiting on the desk.

Hal had done all this in one day. One day! It probably only took a mere snap of the fingers when he had all the Chissolm wealth at his disposal! With bitter irony Karen remembered his meticulous survey of David's room last night. She had scrimped and saved over years to buy what Hal had provided in one day. How could she possibly compete with him?

David was goggle-eyed with wonder for a few moments, then he exploded with excitement. He whirled from one thing to another, touching, trying toys out, and babbling delight at his new father who answered him with happy indulgence. When David ran over to Hal with a mechanical robot he couldn't work, Hal bent down and demonstrated its action on the floor. David was entranced. Hal smiled up at

Karen, a totally unguarded smile inviting her to share the moment with him, but she could not return it. His eyes hardened as he rose to his feet.

'Something wrong?'

'You can't buy love, Hal,' she grated out.

'I'm not trying to.' A bitter edge crept into his voice. 'You had the joy of giving for three birthdays and three Christmases, not to mention David's actual birth. Let's say I'm making up for missed opportunities. Now you can put a smile on your face and stay with us or get out and leave my son with me. Please yourself.'

Hatred welled up inside her. She would not let him take David away from her—never! And at that moment David raced over and grabbed her hand.

'Come and see, Mummy! There's lots and lots of Matchbox cars!'

Karen threw a triumphant look at Hal before accompanying her son, but her only answer was a soft chuckle which gave her an uncomfortable, crawly feeling. She stayed. She sat in the bean-bag and Hal sprawled on the floor next to her, and together they gave David the image of parents in mutual accord, happily indulging their son in a family hour before bedtime. Hal was faultless in his act with her, and Karen was forced to support his role by David's pleasure in having both his mummy and daddy pandering to him.

It was a tremendous relief to Karen when she

could finally declare it was David's bed time. David protested but Hal supported her. He took David into the en-suite bathroom, then stood by joking with him while Karen helped him into his pyjamas and put him into bed. She kissed David goodnight and he looked up at Hal expectantly. The soft compound of love and pleasure on Hal's face as he bent to kiss his son tore at Karen's heart. But David was her son too, her mind cried defensively, and the years of loving gave her more right to him.

'Thanks for all the toys, Daddy,' David mumbled as he snuggled into his pillow.

'You're welcome, son. See you in the morning.'

'See you,' David echoed contentedly.

Hal switched out the light and caught Karen's hand as she brushed past him. He held her fast while he quietly shut the door.

'Let me go!' Karen muttered at him. 'David's not watching now,' she added, resentful of the liberties he had taken under his son's delighted eyes, and all too aware that the advantage had gone to him in this last hour with David.

'From mother to shrew in one quick step,' he mocked. 'I haven't shown you to your room yet, Karen. It's just along here, next door to David's.'

Feeling sick and defeated, Karen allowed him to lead her to her room. Her eyes registered the feminine elegance of the Queen Anne suite and the soft peach tonings of the furnishings,

but the luxurious setting meant nothing to her.
Her mind was fixed on Hal, and with all the
desperation in her heart she attacked the
specious argument he had used for the stance
he was taking.

'How can you say you sacrificed yourself for
Kirsty? She went with you everywhere, sharing
your life and your work and your bed!'

'Did she?' The words were grated back at her
with venom. In an abrupt explosion of violence
Hal slammed the door shut and spun Karen
around to face him, his fingers digging into the
soft flesh of her upper arms, his eyes ablaze
with fierce emotion. 'I'll give you the truth
about Kirsty, Karen. She didn't share—she
took. And I never loved her. I lied to you in the
hospital because I want my son and I'll fight
you for him any way I can. I never loved Kirsty,
but I gave her love. I gave and she took.'

A spasm of pain crossed his face. He dropped
his hands and paced away from Karen, waving
a cutting dismissal. 'She started off as my
partner and she was good, the very best—brave
and fearless, yet with a compassion for others
that made her very vulnerable. She moved me
as no other woman had. She was almost the
woman I wanted and I would have married her,
but Kirsty refused. Yet I knew she needed me. I
believed she loved me . . .

'Kirsty did love you, Hal,' Karen interrupted
softly. 'Maybe she refused to marry you because
she knew you didn't love her.'

He shook his head and swung around, his face screwed into a seething rage of denial. 'How can you say that when she did what she did! I stayed with her! I stayed with her because I sensed that if I didn't, she would become totally reckless. I didn't understand the demons that drove her on, but I can tell you this . . . after she gave my child to you, she plied me to take on more and more dangerous assignments. She became more rash, more adventurous, taking risks that didn't need to be taken. Sometimes she scared the hell out of me.'

'You didn't have to stay,' Karen pointed out quietly.

He looked at her with world-weary eyes. 'Didn't I, Karen? Let me tell you something, if you don't already know it. When someone depends on you, clings to you for emotional support as Kirsty clung to me, and you know that if you don't give it, that person will be destroyed, it takes a more callous man than I am to walk away. I couldn't leave her—even though I wanted to end it, I couldn't leave her. She meant too much to me.'

The picture that he had drawn of Kirsty tore at Karen's heart, but her sister was dead and Karen was fighting for her own life. 'But you're prepared to destroy me!' she shot at Hal.

He lifted his head proudly, shrugging off the grim mantle of the past with ruthless ease. His voice dropped to a silky caress. 'Destroy you, Karen? Not at all. I'm offering you an easy life

of luxury with the son you love.' He strolled
back to her and forcibly held her against him
with one vice-like arm as he stroked her cheek
and ran the long silk of her hair through his
fingers. His eyes held a feverish glitter that
mesmerised Karen into passivity. 'And any
other children we have will have their rightful
father and mother.'

'I haven't . . .' Her mouth was completely
dry. She swallowed hard. 'I haven't said I'll
marry you.'

'But you will, Karen, you will. You know, as
Kirsty lay dying in my arms, she talked of you,
Karen. Not about my being with her, not about
what she and I had together, it was all about
you! She took from me and she gave to you. So I
figure it's about time I did some taking.'

And he kissed her with a devastating
deliberation that left Karen feeling more
helpless than ever, because she wanted to
respond. Whether it was his very male physical
magnetism, or the softening effect of the
emotional support he had given Kirsty, or the
fact that she was too drained to resist, Karen
did not know. But she was quivering inside
when the kiss ended.

'Dinner will be in ten minutes,' Hal said
calmly. 'Don't be late down.'

He left her—just like that. With all the
arrogant carelessness of a man who had seen to
business and knew that everything was in hand.

Karen wrapped her arms around her body

and helplessly, hopelessly, tried to fight off the strands of circumstance which seemed to be binding her to a man she didn't love, and who certainly did not love her.

CHAPTER SEVEN

IT WAS almost over. The two nights and two days at the Chissolm home had strained Karen's nerves to the limit, and even now, back in her own home, she could not relax until Hal left. David had pleaded for 'Daddy' to stay and help put him to bed. Karen had given in to the plea, just as she had been giving in all weekend, but with David finally settled for the night, she could not get Hal out of the house fast enough. As he silently followed her to the front door, she felt strained by the pressure his very presence exerted.

She had evaded being alone with him since that kiss on Friday night. In front of David or Owen, Hal had treated her with charm and the utmost courtesy, but there had been a few private moments when that mask had slipped and ruthless calculation had stared her in the face. They were alone now, and as Karen held the door open she used it as a half-shield between her and Hal.

He paused beside her, a sardonic little smile telling her that the manoeuvre had not gone unnoticed. Karen stiffened, determined to repel any move he made towards her. Despite a physical attraction which she could not deny, his touch was too disturbing for her to take any pleasure from it. Hal did not like her or want her, but she was all too aware that he was intent on taking her.

'You have until Thursday night, Karen. You either say yes to marriage or you'll lose David.'

'Can't you see he needs both of us?' she fired back hotly.

There was no melting in those ice-cold grey eyes. 'Yes,' he replied, totally unperturbed. 'There really isn't any other answer but marriage, is there?'

He walked away and Karen shut the door, but she could not shut his exit line out of her mind. She fought against it, railed against it, but there was a terrible inevitability about it which made her determined opposition seem futile.

And the sense of inevitability grew, weighing even more heavily on her heart on Monday morning as her solicitor droned through his view of the case. Mr Grimball was a big man with many chins, a balding head and bright brown eyes. The last time Karen had visited him he had been bluff and hearty and comfortably reassuring. His eyes had twinkled with kindly indulgence. Today the eyes seemed shifty, and his manner was decidedly shifty.

'There are two things worse than your ex-husband's evidence, Mrs Aylward. Ex-husbands . . .' he wriggled his fingers, ". . . well, they can have reasons for giving evidence against ex-wives.'

'And what are the two things worse?' Karen prompted. Mr Grimball was doing a lot of shifting off the point.

'Yes. Well, they might put you in the witness box, Mrs Aylward. There's your reply to the question—did your sister tell you that Hal Chissolm was David's father? Can you deny it?'

'No.'

He pushed his bottom lip forward and lowered his eyebrows. Then with suggestive deliberation he asked, 'Will you deny it?'

'No.'

His shrug was all too eloquent. 'And one can't get around your sister's evidence, dead though she may be. I don't know whether people do or do not lie when they are dying, but no court is going to believe that Kirsty Balfour was lying when she told Mr Chissolm he was David's father only a few minutes before she died. These cases are not based on reasonable doubt, but on the balance of probabilities. Even with reasonable doubt we would have problems. In this case . . .' He threw up his hands.

'So there's no hope,' Karen concluded for him.

'There's always hope, Mrs Aylward, but on balance, I think we should do what we can to settle this matter out of court. Get whatever we can, and the sooner the better. Nothing is certain with the law, and I've won worse cases than the one they have, Mrs Aylward.'

No hope! And no hope of settling out of court either. She had four days to decide on the future—marriage or a legal fight that would make David the bone between two dogs, with herself the probable loser. Although they would all lose, Karen thought grimly. She heaved a sigh and rose to her feet.

'Thank you, Mr Grimball. I'll give you my decision shortly.'

He billowed out of his chair and fussed over her to the door, mouthing platitudes and warnings. She nodded and nodded, but her mind was already leaping ahead. A judge would grant her access to David, there was no doubt about that. But she knew that Hal would fight to make it as limited an access as possible. And as Mr Grimball said, nothing was certain with the law. The only certainty which would keep David in her life in any meaningful way was marriage to Hal.

Her thoughts drifted over the marriage she had experienced with Barry as she headed towards the closest shopping centre. She had been a bride at nineteen, even before she had completed her teacher's training course. Barry had been twenty-five, handsome, exciting, very sure of himself and her. She had thought herself in love with him and he had swept her into marriage while she had still been dazzled by his image.

Barry had always been a man's man, although Karen hadn't realised what that meant until they were married. His ego was bound up in male competitiveness, being a better squash player than his mates, owning a sportier car, having a prettier, smarter wife. It was pride in his masculinity that had been shattered with the news that he could not father a family. That was why he had gone out after other women. Karen had forgiven him that, and although she had felt disappointed in their relationship, she would have stuck by him if he had accepted David. His failure to do so had completed her disillusionment in their marriage.

She had been a weak fool to let him persuade her into tonight's meeting. It would not matter what important thing he had to tell her, there was no way she wanted to resume a relationship with him. If he cared so much about her, he should have contacted her before giving that statement to Hal's lawyers. He had to have known what it meant to her, and he surely knew she would not want to lose David. She did not expect him to perjure himself, but he need not have given that statement, without even warning her! He had no consideration for her feelings at all.

Karen stared down at the packet of pasta she had picked up from the supermarket shelf. Here she was buying food to make Barry an Italian meal, because he liked Italian food, so she was automatically going out of her way to

please him, just as she always had. She shook
her head but dropped the packet into her
shopping trolley. Old habits died hard. Besides,
it was easy enough to cook lasagne.

When Karen collected David from the next-
door neighbour who had kindly consented to
mind him for the morning, she had to face a
number of good-natured questions. David had
been talking about his weekend with 'Daddy'.
David adored 'Daddy'. Karen backed off as
politely as she could, giving a few vague
answers before hurrying David away, but there
was no escape from David. He raved on about
'Daddy' for the rest of the day, giving Karen no
peace from thoughts of Hal. The only relief
came when she put David to bed, and then
there was only half an hour left before Barry
was due to arrive.

Her head was whirling with her dilemma.
She was in no mood to cope with a visit from
her ex-husband. Barry hadn't wanted David,
but Hal did. But Karen didn't want either man.
She just wanted to be left alone with the little
boy she had mothered since he had been born.

Barry presented himself with a bottle of
champagne, as if the occasion was something to
celebrate. Karen's heart sank even further.
There was no cause for her to celebrate. She led
him into the living room, provided the necessary glasses and watched him with jaundiced
eyes as he opened the bottle. Maybe it was the
problem of David weighing on her mind, but

she found that she felt nothing for the man to whom she had been married for so long. Which seemed wrong. There should have been something from the years they had spent together.

He looked good, yet she could not even feel attracted to him any more. He was dressed to impress in a well-tailored brown suit and a cream silk shirt. There were streaks of grey in his curly brown hair which had not been there two years ago but they added to his air of confident maturity. He was as tall as Hal and his physique was more solid, yet he did not impart the same innate strength. There seemed almost a soft self-indulgence in the fleshier face. But at least there was warmth in the blue eyes as Barry passed her a glass brimming with champagne.

'You look great, Karen,' he said with fervour.

A ripple of guilt for her lack of fervour forced a responsive smile. 'You look in fine fettle yourself, Barry. Tell me what you've been doing over the last two years.'

He told her—all through dinner. He was so full of his doings, he didn't get around to asking about hers. Karen thanked him for the compliments he gave her and fed him more questions, but there was only one question pounding through her mind, and finally she could not hold it in any longer. He hadn't asked her about David; he had not even mentioned David. But

David was the only issue that Karen could think about.

'Why did you sign that statement for Hal Chissolm's lawyers, Barry?' she asked bluntly.

He frowned and looked uncomfortable. 'Because it was the truth, Karen. We both know that.'

Yes, they both knew that, but Barry's lack of consideration for her still grated. 'You didn't have to lie. You could have remained silent. Don't you realise they're trying to take David away from me?'

'Karen . . .' he reached over and took her hand, his mouth curved into a persuasive smile, '. . . forget David for a moment. I want to talk about us. I've got good news to tell you.'

Her inner anxiety was too great to put aside. She had listened and listened to Barry for well over an hour. She needed him to listen to her. 'I can't forget David, Barry. Didn't you hear what I said? They're going to take him away from me.'

'Dammit, Karen, the boy should be with his natural father anyway! He came between us before, breaking up our marriage. It's better if he goes. It'd give us a clean start again.'

Karen stared at him, too appalled to speak. How could she have ever thought that she had loved this man? He had no feelings, no sensitivities beyond himself. He had left her with a child that he had agreed to adopt. She had lived for and loved that child for three

years without any support from him, and now
he expected her to dismiss David as though it
should mean nothing to her.

'Just listen, Karen,' he insisted, dropping his
voice to earnest entreaty. 'I can have children
now. There's a new technigue of sperm concentration. It will involve you in a laparotomy but I
know you won't mind that. We can have
children of our own, Karen. There's never
really been anyone else for me, no one I would
want as my wife. I want us to get married again,
Karen, have the life together that we planned
in the first place.'

'But you want me to give David up,' she
whispered, hardly able to believe that he could
ask her to wash her hands of a child whom she
loved.

'Don't you see, Karen? We'll have children
of our own,' he repeated eagerly. 'It's what we
always wanted, dreamed of and planned for. I
know I shouldn't have left you, but the love you
showered on David made me so jealous of what
we couldn't have that I couldn't stand it. It was
tearing me apart—I had to leave. You must
forgive me for that, Karen.'

Tearing him apart. Yes, she could see that
now. His inability to accept another man's son
was part and parcel of his character. And for
her to love any child but Barry's would always
be unacceptable. 'There's nothing to forgive,
Barry,' she said flatly. 'I guess it wasn't all your
fault. I didn't love you enough to understand

what was happening to you. So I was selfish as well as you.'

He squeezed her hand in happy relief. 'You weren't selfish, Karen—you were never that. Let me court you again. We'll enjoy ourselves, pick up the threads of our life, and things will be better than they ever were before. And when you're ready we'll get married again.'

On his terms. It would never be any other way; Barry was blind to any feelings but his own. Karen withdrew her hand and struggled to answer him kindly. 'I'm very pleased for your sake, Barry, to hear your good news—I really am. But I can't marry you again.'

He was puzzled. 'But you said you've forgiven me.' She heaved a sigh and looked at him with bleak eyes. 'It has nothing to do with the past, Barry. I simply can't share your future.'

'Why not?' he demanded almost truculently.

He wouldn't understand; he was too wrapped up in himself to understand. She gave him an answer which had no comeback. 'Because I'm going to marry Hal Chissolm.'

'Hal Chissolm!' His face ran a gamut of emotions from astonishment to resentment. 'You'd marry your own sister's lover?'

Karen flinched. Barry had found a comeback all right, and it was a stab to the heart. 'Kirsty is dead, Barry.'

He flushed. That was another subject he had avoided tonight, and Karen remembered belatedly that Kirsty had never liked Barry—she had said as much after the divorce.

'You can't love him!' Barry blustered. 'He's only just returned to Australia. What do you want to marry him for?'

'That's my business, Barry.'

He glared at her. 'I suppose it's his money!'

Karen pushed back her chair and stood up, very much on her dignity. 'I'd like you to leave now, Barry. We really don't have anything more to say. I do wish you well, but there's no point in our seeing each other again.'

He rose to his feet, anger making his face almost ugly. 'It's that bloody kid of his, isn't it? That's why you're marrying him—to keep your precious David! You sacrificed our marriage for Hal Chissolm's bastard kid, and now you're going to sacrifice yourself. It's crazy, can't you see that? Let the boy go, for God's sake!'

'I can't do that, Barry. I'm his mother. Now please . . .'

'Kirsty was his mother!' he raged, then made an effort to pull himself together. 'You've got this thing all cockeyed, Karen. I thought that having gone it on your own for a few years and seen how tough it was, you'd be only too glad to get rid of David when he'd be going to a better home. I signed that statement because it was good for both of us. Hal Chissolm wants the boy. It's natural that he'll love his son. It's time you . . .'

'Don't say any more, Barry. Just go,' she

commanded coldly. 'I don't love you. I don't want to marry you, so no purpose can be served by your staying here any longer.'

The anger he had striven to control blazed out again. 'You're nothing but a damned fool, Karen!' he shouted at her, then stormed out of the house, slamming the door after him.

Karen sank back on to her chair, propped her elbows on the dining-table and covered her face with her hands. So she was a fool for thinking of marrying Hal Chissolm, and she would probably suffer a private damnation if she did marry him, but what else could she do? She didn't want a life without David, nor a life where she only saw him for brief periods. She wanted to be there for him day by day, watching over his growing up. He was her son. Kirsty's son. Hal's son.

Kirsty had loved Hal; Karen did not understand her sister's decision or actions, but she was certain that Kirsty had loved Hal. And under the hard shell of hurt which was driving him to take such a ruthless payment for what had been done, Hal was a good man, a giving man. He had stayed with Kirsty until her death and he would be a loving father to David— Karen could not doubt that after seeing him with David over the weekend. Maybe, in time, he would soften towards her.

To Karen's weary mind it seemed inevitable that she should marry him. Kirsty, Hal, David and herself . . . the connections were too close, too intertwined for any escape from them. There was no point in waiting until Thursday before giving him her decision. Nothing was going to change. Nothing could change. And with that thought came a pleasantly numb peace of mind.

She dragged herself up from the table, walked out to the family room, picked up the telephone and dialled. Her hands were quite steady. Her voice was also steady as she asked to speak to Hal. When he answered, she felt an odd satisfaction in hearing his voice.

'Karen? What can I do for you?'

It was a hard voice, a strong voice, without any of Barry's persuasive tone. Yet the question pleased her. 'What can I do for you?' Barry had not asked that question tonight, not once, for all that he had said he loved her. Karen took a deep breath.

'I've decided to marry you, Hal.'

There was a short silence, then, 'It was the only sensible choice. I'll make an appointment at the Register Office for Friday afternoon.'

That startled her. 'This Friday afternoon? But . . .'

'I've already made arrangements for a special licence to be pushed through. My solicitor will be around to see you tomorrow to get your signature on the relevant documents.'

Had he been so sure of her decision? 'I won't be here tomorrow, Hal—I have to go to work.'

'Give it a miss. Or get leave of absence. Or

resign. You don't have to work any more, Karen.'

Her backbone stiffened. She might be marrying him, but he wasn't going to take over her whole life. 'I prefer to work, thank you. And David comes to work with me.'

'As you like,' Hal conceded carelessly. 'Do you want to sell your house or rent it?'

'I haven't thought about it.' He was throwing so much at her that Karen's mind was whirling again.

'I'll send my solicitor around to the kindergarten to see you. He's good. Tell him what you want done with the house. I'll let you know what time for the Register Office on Friday,' Hal concluded matter-of-factly.

'Yes. Thank you.'

'Goodnight, Karen.'

'Goodnight,' she echoed limply.

The line went dead and Karen slowly replaced her receiver. The die was cast now. She would be married to Hal Chissolm on Friday. So final so soon, yet if it was to be done, it was probably better that it be done quickly. She lifted her chin to a proud, defiant angle. If she was going to Hal as a sacrifice, he would not find a head bowed in submission.

CHAPTER EIGHT

THERE had been so much to do that Karen had found it relatively easy not to think about what marriage to Hal would mean to her personally. She had simply blocked it out, driving herself along with constant activity during the day until she fell into bed at night, so physically exhausted that sleep was almost immediate. By Friday morning all the cleaning of the house and the packing had been completed to her satisfaction and there was nothing left to do but think.

The normal kind of marriage, Hal had said— which meant sharing his bed. Her mind kept skittering away from that thought, but it could not be banished. The only man she had ever been with was Barry. Would it be very different with Hal? Could she cope with such physical intimacy where there was no semblance of love? Did he intend to take her as ruthlessly as he had driven her into this marriage? Would he be thinking of Kirsty?

For some reason it was this last question which upset Karen most. Physically she was Kirsty's double and she could not forget that her sister had shared Hal's bed for six years. Never in her life had Karen wished that she was not Kirsty's identical twin, but she wished it now, quite desperately.

She was in no state to face Owen when he arrived to pick up David. Hal had arranged that David spend the day with his grandfather. Karen had not seen Owen or spoken with him since the previous weekend, so she had no idea how he viewed this hasty marriage, nor did she want to talk about it with him now. No matter what Owen thought, she had to go through with it.

She met him at the door and evaded his sharp blue eyes when he greeted her, quickly bending down to give David a last hug before he went. 'Be a good boy for Pop now,' she murmured huskily, fighting to hold back a sudden rush of tears.

'Go on out to the car, David. Harper's there and he has something for you. I just want a word with your mother,' Owen said firmly.

David was off with a skip of excitement before Karen had even straightened up. She watched him go through a blur of tears. He was so happy. She could not say or do anything to mar that innocent happiness. She lifted her face reluctantly to Owen's.

His expression was hard and bleak and his words did nothing to ease the turmoil in her mind. 'I've liked you from the first time we've met, Karen. I couldn't believe Hal when he told me what you were doing. I know how you felt about Hal and I don't think those feelings could have changed so radically in so short a time. Whatever reason you have for making this marriage, it's inadequate, and I fear you'll both regret it.'

He didn't know the truth, and he was misjudging her. Stung by a sense of injustice, Karen was about to straighten him out when David called to her, waving a model aeroplane in childish glee. The few moments' distraction gave her time for second thoughts. Owen loved Hal as deeply as she loved David. Kirsty had inadvertently driven a wedge between father and son, and Karen did not want to widen the gap. Owen had been good to her and her commitment to Hal was already binding enough to demand some loyalty. If Hal did not want his father to know the truth, then it was not her place to tell him.

Her eyes held a bitter sadness as she turned back to him. This marriage was giving no one any joy—except David. 'I'm doing what I think is necessary, Owen,' she said quietly.

He subjected her to an intense scrutiny which did nothing to soothe her jangled nerves. Finally he shook his head in disbelief and strode down the path, disapproval radiating from his stiff back. Karen sagged a little as the Rolls Royce drove away. It hurt that Owen's good opinion of her had been shaken. She liked him, far more than she liked his son. But it was Hal she was marrying.

The carrier arrived soon afterwards, and

Karen pointed out the boxes of personal effects to be taken. Although the rooms were still furnished, they looked bare and characterless when she walked through them, checking that nothing important was left behind. She had the sensation that her whole life up to this point had been put into storage, and nothing would ever be the same again.

Left alone once more, Karen put a mental clamp on her thoughts. It was her wedding day, even if the wedding was a travesty of what it should be. She showered and settled down to indulging herself with a slow, thorough toilet; hair brushed to shiny bounciness, nails varnished a soft coral, make-up applied with meticulous care. The cream woollen suit was the most expensive outfit she had bought for years, but pride had dictated that she go to Hal with her head held high. The coral silk blouse was a defiant splash of colour which denied the drab feeling in her soul.

A hire car called for her at the designated time. The driver picked up the small overnight bag which was all that was left to be taken. She had no intimation of Hal's intentions after the wedding, except that they would pick up David once the formalities had been completed. She had had no personal communication from Hal since Monday night; everything had been organised through his solicitor. She locked the front door for the last time and followed the driver out to the car, each step requiring more and more determined courage.

Hal was waiting for her outside the Register Office. His dark, pin-striped suit seemed to be a gesture to the formality of the occasion. There was no friendly smile of greeting from him, and he looked grim and purposeful as he helped Karen out of the car. When the driver offered him the overnight bag he gave a curt instruction and turned Karen away, almost hurrying her into the building.

The terrible emptiness in Karen's stomach gave birth to a flock of fluttering butterflies. She barely heard the words of ceremony, but she was overwhelmingly conscious of the man who stood next to her. She did not, could not love Hal Chissolm, but she knew why Kirsty had found him irresistible. He exuded assurance, a deadliness and inexorability of ruthless purpose that both fascinated and repelled. In a strange, incomprehensible way it steadied her, and her hand was quite nerveless as she signed away her life, committing herself into his keeping.

Only then did Hal turn her towards him and kiss her, just a light brushing of his lips against hers, yet it made her heart thump at an accelerated rate. 'Till death us do part,' he murmured, his eyes mocking the uncertainty in hers.

The mention of death gave her stomach a queasy turn. Hal had stayed with Kirsty until her death, and it was Kirsty's dying words which had tied this knot between them. Karen could not help wondering if Hal was thinking of her sister as they left the Register Office—the woman who had refused to marry him, the identical twin of the woman he had just married. Karen could read nothing in his face. He wore the same hard, implacable mask he had shown her on the night he had first proposed this marriage.

He led her to a green Porsche which looked new. 'Your wedding present,' he announced drily. 'Want to drive it?'

'My . . .' Karen shook her head in dazed bewilderment. 'You're giving this to me?'

'You'll need it, since you insist on taking David to work with you. Come on, I'll show you how to drive it.'

Even though Hal had obviously bought the car for David more than for her, the gift lifted her spirits. The concentration required to follow Hal's instructions also precluded more disturbing thoughts. The drive to Turramurra was fraught with mechanical pitfalls rather than emotional ones, but their arrival at Owen Chissolm's home brought tension screaming back. Karen fumbled with her seat-belt, suddenly all thumbs.

Hal's hand closed over hers. 'Leave it on. I'll go and get David.'

She lifted startled eyes to his 'Where are we going?' she queried.

A faint smile curved his mouth. 'To our new home. Where else?'

A new home. Karen's heart contracted. Despite Owen's disapproval this morning, she had taken comfort from the thought that his presence might ease some of the strain in the relationship between herself and Hal, but a new home meant there would only be Hal. And David, she reminded herself quickly, trying to quell her inner panic.

In a matter of minutes Hal was back with David, who was full of excitement; impressed with the new car, entranced with the idea of going to a new home, and most of all, delighted that he was going to live with Daddy as well as Mummy. Apart from the directions he casually threw to Karen, Hal gave all his attention to his son. It was as if she was travelling with a different man, he was so relaxed and happy.

He had got what he had set out to achieve, Karen reasoned despondently. It was impossible for her to relax; she was too full of apprehension about what this new life would mean to her. Hal finally pointed to a driveway which led to a house of awesome proportions. It overlooked the glittering expanse of Pittwater, and Karen did not need telling that the real estate alone was worth a fortune.

It was not a mansion like Owen's home, but as Hal led Karen through the double-door entrance she knew she had never seen a more luxurious house. Huge glass areas provided a commanding view of the flotilla of sailing boats that skimmed across Pittwater. The carpets were thick, the rooms huge, the furniture all the best of modern design. It was a house which not only contained beautiful entertaining areas, but which had cosy living areas also. Karen particularly liked the sunny breakfast room and the television room.

'You won't have to worry about housekeeping,' Hal told her casually. 'There's a couple, Mr and Mrs Hanley, who live in an apartment on the lower level. He's the gardener and general handyman, and she keeps the house in order. You'll meet them on Monday.'

Karen nodded, too overwhelmed to speak. She supposed she would get used to it all in time. David was in seventh heaven, racing around, discovering all the novelties of his new home. Hal led them upstairs and presented David's room to him. It was virtually a replica of the room he had provided in Owen's home, and the toys that he had bought were all here for David's pleasure.

'Your mother and I are going to change into more comfortable clothes,' Hal told him matter-of-factly. 'Will you be happy playing here?'

David had just spilled the box of Lego on to the floor. He looked up with dancing eyes. 'I'll build up a big space station, Daddy!'

Hal grinned. 'You do that, son. I'll be back to see it in a little while.'

David was already too busy to answer, and

Hal turned Karen away, steering her down the
hallway to another room. It was obviously the
master bedroom, and Karen's gaze skittered
away from the king-size bed which she would
have to share with him tonight. Her luggage
was stacked near an opened doorway which led
to a dressing room. The carpet was a pale lemon
and the furnishings were mainly gold and
white.

Nervous of being alone with Hal, Karen
walked over to pull the curtains back from a
row of glass doors. Another view of Pittwater
sparkled at her, but she did not enjoy it. She was
far too aware that Hal was discarding his tie,
his jacket, and his waistcoat. She willed him to
move into the dressing room before he discarded more clothes.

He moved, but not to the dressing room. He
strolled up behind her, and before she realised
what he intended his hands closed around her
waist and pulled her back against him. Shock
rippled through her as his fingers began
unbuttoning her jacket.

'What . . . what are you doing?' she choked
out.

'Undressing you, since you don't seem
inclined to undress yourself.'

As his fingers started on her blouse buttons,
sheer panic drove Karen to twist around in his
embrace. Fear feathered down her spine as she
caught the broodingly intent look on his face.

'You can't mean . . . not . . . not now,' she

stammered, her heart in her mouth.

'Why not? We're married. For better, for worse, remember? And I want it better, Karen.' He pulled her closer and his lips pressed warm kisses to her temples. 'Better than anything I've had before.'

'No! We can't!' she cried in frightened protest. 'David might want us.'

'He'll be happy for half an hour.'

His fingers threaded through her hair and tilted her head back. His mouth took hers in a passionate demand which almost drained her of any will at all. He pressed her body even closer to his, leaving her in no doubt that he was sexually aroused. Karen jerked her head back, gasping for breath.

'No! Later, Hal. Tonight,' she pleaded, struggling to deny that she could be responding to his desire.

The grey eyes glittered with purpose. 'That too, Karen. But I want you now.'

And there was no stopping him. He wouldn't take no for an answer. Karen trembled with a sense of inevitability as his fingers flicked open the last button and he slid both jacket and blouse from her shoulders. For a few moments she went completely limp, but she found it impossible to remain passive as his mouth roamed down her throat, across her shoulder, down to the soft swell of her breasts. Her skin leapt in sharp tingles of excitement.

She told herself she shouldn't be reacting like

this, but even as Hal whirled her around and laid her on the end of the bed to remove the rest of her clothes she could not quell a shiver of anticipation. He was so aggressively masculine, emanating an urgency which communicated itself to her. His eyes raked her naked body as he stripped himself of his own clothes, and Karen writhed inside at her utter vulnerability. She turned her gaze away, wishing it could be different between them, wishing there could be caring and love in the union Hal was forcing.

She cried out as he touched her, an instinctive cry of protest against the intimacy he was taking, but his mouth smothered any further cry and his body pinned her down, making any struggle futile while the offending hand caressed her into trembling acceptance. He kissed her with such fierce passion that Karen could do nothing but give herself up to it, and once he sensed her submission Hal moved to take complete possession.

She looked up at him, feeling hopelessly lost to all that she believed was right. There was no love between them, yet as his gaze met and locked with hers, a compelling hunger throbbed between them, unspoken yet reflected in each other's eyes. Hal's face was strained with the need to go on, and she knew her own face was tight with tension. For a moment he hesitated, a look of pain darkening the need, then with a harsh, guttural cry he drove himself deep inside her.

A wild, primitive elation burst through her, an incomprehensible, savage response to Hal's savagery. He plunged into her again and again, long, hard strokes that thrust for a dominance which she denied him by moving with the rhythm, inviting, goading him on with a wantonness she did not stop to question. Never in her life had she experienced anything like this before, this sense of ecstatic oneness in an act of mutual possession. Her body was exulting in it, adjusting itself to new levels of almost unendurable pleasure.

Karen closed her eyes, concentrating all her being on the inner world which was pulsing towards an exquisite tension. Hal's arms slid under her hips, lifting her higher. Then with one deep, explosive thrust, there came a sudden flooding of warmth which spread a blissful peace throughout her whole body. She ceased to move, utterly transfixed by a fulfilment she had never known, and her eyes opened in dazed wonder, needing to see the man who had done this.

His body was arched back. Beads of perspiration lined his forehead. Still he held her hard against his loins and his breath came in deep, rough gasps. He shuddered, and Karen felt his release, a wave of warmth joining and mingling with hers, and suddenly their union lost its magic and she felt shamed by her participation in what could never be called an act of love.

How could she have made the highly

abandoned response she had made? It was so wanton, with a man who had forced his will on her. Resentment curdled the pleasure he had given her. Her soul cried out for some revenge for the ravaging of her sensibilities.

'If you're quite satisfied, I'd like to get up and go to David,' she said coldly.

His eyes opened and shot her a look of incredulity before anger wiped it out. He let her go, his body moving so abruptly from hers that Karen felt strangely bereft. He stood up, tall, masculine and menacing as he towered over her. Rage suffused his face and she could see the effort he had to make not to attack her physically. His hands clenched and unclenched as he fought for control. His eyes were like diamond needles, cutting into her flesh. Fear clutched at Karen's heart. She regretted the rejection she had just slapped in his face. They were married, she had to live with him. She should have accepted the fact that she could respond to him with relief.

Hal's hand reached out and lightly fanned her breast, making her nipple tingle to an erect excitement. His fingers feathered over her stomach and down one thigh. Her sensitised skin shivered with pleasure, but she shrank from his touch, still ashamed that he could so easily arouse a response from her.

'Don't think you can deny either yourself or me, Karen. It won't work—not until you're pregnant, anyway. Then I might be satisfied.'

He turned his back on her and strode into the dressing room, re-emerging a few minutes later in dark blue corduroy slacks and a red sweater. He walked straight through the bedroom without even glancing at her and closed the door after him with a decisive click.

Karen had pulled the quilt around her, but Hal's words had chilled her to the bone and she felt too frozen to move. Was that his revenge? To get her pregnant so that he would have the full experience of fathering a child? Had he only taken her for that reason?

She shuddered and hugged the quilt more closely around her. It couldn't be just that, she reasoned unhappily. He had kissed her with passion, taken her with passion. He had wanted her—whether because she looked like Kirsty or not, she didn't know, but he had wanted her. And she had wanted him, she admitted to herself in sick misery. There was something about Hal which answered some deep need in her. Against all reason it was there, and she could not deny it.

She wished she had held her tongue and waited for him to say something. She remembered the look in his eyes just before he had taken her. Maybe it had been a need for love too. Had he felt the same strange fulfilment in their union? Had she ruined any chance they might have had of reaching out to each other in any but a physical sense?

It was getting dark. She had to move; David

would be wondering where she was. Or would he? David had Hal now. A wave of lonely desolation drove Karen from the bed. She found an *ensuite* bathroom off the dressing room and had a quick shower, feeling too self-conscious of her body to stay under the hot spray for very long. She dressed in her comfortable stretch jeans and a brightly patterned sloppy joe, then unpacked her suitcases, moving quickly to put everything away before facing up to Hal again. Somehow it made her feel more positive. This was her home now.

She found David and Hal in the kitchen, which was superbly designed with every modern aid to cooking. Hal was beating eggs and David gleefully informed her that Daddy was making an omelette for his tea. On the surface the next hour and a half passed very pleasantly, with David unaware of the underlying tension between his parents. He went to bed in a mood of happy contentment which Karen privately envied.

Hal was good with his son, indulgent until firm authority was needed and then making that authority felt without even raising his voice. Karen wondered if he could be as good a husband as he was a father. As he was a lover, a traitorous little voice added.

There were steaks in the refrigerator, and Karen cooked them for dinner while Hal mixed a salad. Neither of them spoke except to ask about preferences in the food they were preparing. Hal opened a bottle of wine, and they sat at the table in the breakfast room, both automatically shunning the more romantic setting of the formal dining room.

Hating the prickly silence which had grown between them, Karen asked Hal what work he would be doing from now on. He replied at length, prompted by more questions from her. She could almost pretend it was a normal conversation, but not quite. The gentle mockery in the grey eyes kept reminding her of all that was being left unsaid. The final silencer was the memory that Kirsty had shared Hal's work in a way that Karen never could.

Tears stung Karen's eyes. It was hopeless to even think she could forge a successful relationship with Hal; Kirsty would always stand between them in one way or another. Karen quickly downed the last of her wine and stood up, stacking the plates in quick order. She carried them out to the kitchen and put them in the dishwasher.

'It's been a long day. If you'll excuse me, I think I'll go to bed,' she threw at Hal, who had followed her.

'Go ahead,' he answered carelessly.

She virtually bolted up the stairs in her need to escape from him before she broke down entirely. She could feel herself snapping under all the tensions of the day, and she only just managed to get the bedroom door closed before the floodgates opened. She wept copious, bitter tears as she blindly undressed, pulled on a nightdress and crawled into bed. She curled herself into a self-protective ball and buried her face in a pillow, but she could not stifle the sobs that kept welling from the ache in her heart.

She did not see or hear Hal come in. The first she knew of his presence was the gentle, smoothing caress on her tangled hair. She jerked away and twisted around to fend him off, unable to bear his touch.

'I'm not Kirsty!' she cried, her emotions too torn to keep silent.

'No, you're not,' came the soft reply.

He was sitting on the bed, but it was too dark for her to discern his expression. He stood up and pulled off his sweater.

'Can't you leave me alone?' she begged.

He stepped out of his trousers, and as he climbed into bed with her Karen turned her back to him, frightened by the chaotic pumping of her heart. He did not attempt to pull her into an embrace. He stroked her hair and her back with a gentleness which utterly confused her. She lay very still, wanting to believe the tenderness in his soothing caresses and all too aware of the warmth emanating from his body, although it was only his hand which was touching her. Hal heaved a sigh and slowly curved his body around hers. His hand slid around her waist, while his mouth brushed over her hair.

'I can't say I'm sorry, Karen—I'm not. But

don't think I'm comparing you to Kirsty in any way. There's no comparison.'

Tears flooded into her eyes again. 'You mean I could never match up to my sister.'

'No, that's not what I mean.' He moved, rolling her towards him. He leaned over her and brushed his lips against hers. 'You're different. And I'm different with you. There is no comparison,' he repeated, and kissed her with a slow sensuality that robbed Karen of any thought at all.

Her hands crept up over his back, and in the close darkness of night, she surrendered to the pleasure of following her instincts which encouraged Hal to take whatever he wanted of her. But this time he gave far more than he took, and if it wasn't love, it left Karen feeling as if she had been loved, and she fell asleep, cradled in his arms, a smile of contentment still on her lips.

CHAPTER NINE

IT WAS crazy. It was unreasonable. The highly dubious foundation of their marriage should have discouraged any such feeling from developing, but it had happened. Karen was in love with Hal Chissolm. She knew it was madness, but she simply could not help herself. It was beyond her control.

It was impossible to actually pinpoint the time when her life had stopped revolving around David and started revolving around Hal, but as the weeks had passed her awareness of him had grown until he was now the focus of practically everything she did and thought and felt. She did not understand why it should be so. Barry had never inspired such a depth of feeling even when he had been at his most loving, and Hal certainly didn't love her.

He was kind and considerate to her. The savagery he had shown her on their wedding day had never been repeated. Nor did he mock her efforts to keep a smoothly running relationship with him. He co-operated all the way. But he kept a distance between them that she couldn't cross, no matter how hard she tried.

Sometimes the distance wasn't so apparent. Sometimes she could pretend it wasn't there at all. It frightened her that just a pleasant word or a hard look from him could swing her emotions from happiness to despair. The need to be loved by him was eating into her more each day, and there was nothing she could do to stop it. She tried to hide her vulnerability from him, but she wasn't sure she was successful.

She didn't want to be with anyone else and Hal seemed content with their small family unit. Although he spoke of friends at work he invited no one home, and it came as a jolt when he finally suggested such an invitation, an invitation that Karen found particularly unwelcome.

'My father has been complaining that he hasn't seen anything of David since we were married.'

Hal's casual remark over the dinner table dimmed Karen's pleasant glow of well-being. She had been savouring the companionable tone of their conversation and imagining that they were any normal husband and wife, chatting over the doings of the day. The mention of Owen recalled all too clearly the circumstances of their marriage.

'It's been five weeks,' Hal added with a rueful little smile. 'I thought we could invite him over for lunch on Sunday. Is that all right with you?'

It wasn't all right at all. She did not like the idea of their relationship being put under Owen's critical scrutiny. The memory of his

unjust disapproval of her decision to marry Hal
still had the power to hurt.

'Some problem?'

The slight edge to Hal's voice cut through her
thoughts, and she glanced up quickly to find the
smile gone and the familiar hard reserve in his
eyes.

'No, of course not,' she denied swiftly.
'Sunday lunch is fine.'

But her answer had come too late. The
reserve did not go away and the friendly mood
was spoilt. Hal continued with polite conversation, but it wasn't the same; he had distanced
himself from her again. Karen's happiness
deflated into a dull inner misery as she tried
unsuccessfully to reach past the barrier he had
erected between them.

She hated it when that reserve shuttered his
eyes, closing her out. The best times were when
they took David on a family outing, which they
had done every Sunday; to the beach, to the
zoo, to fantasy playgrounds around the out-
skirts of Sydney. These occasions invariably
provided moments when the love Hal gave
openly to David seemed to be transferred to
Karen in an unguarded look of intimate
sharing.

There were no such moments when he was
alone with her, but occasionally he was relaxed
and friendly, as he had been tonight before her
hesitation over Owen's invitation. Sometimes
Karen wished she could see the expression in

his eyes after they had made love, but it was always too dark. Hal did not touch her during the day except for ordinary courtesies.

More and more Karen regretted her rejection of him that first afternoon. Perhaps it was only a sexual act to him, a necessary process to get her pregnant, yet it never felt like that to her. Hal did not finish with her once he had climaxed, nor did he ever take her without concern for her pleasure. She always fell asleep feeling they were truly one, yet in the morning the barriers were up as if they had never been dropped for a moment.

Just as the barriers were up now, impenetrable. Karen gave up trying to reach past them and retired to the kitchen, taking her frustration out on the pots and pans from dinner. She wished there was some ironing to do, any mundane physical activity that might soothe the turbulence of her thoughts, but the household was run with meticulous efficiency by the housekeeper Hal employed.

Mr and Mrs Hanley were well past middle age and they were both pleasant, cheerful people who liked to be kept busy and took a pride in their work. The garden was always immaculate, the house spotless, and Karen only had to make a list and the shopping was done. All she had to do during the weekdays was cook, and Mrs Hanley even prepared the vegetables for dinner. At the weekends Hal often took charge of the meals, surprising

Karen with his skill until he explained that his tours overseas had taught him how to look after himself.

That was part of the problem with Hal, Karen thought despondently. He didn't need her for anything, except as David's mother, and possibly in his bed. If only he could come to love her as she loved him, she would be so happy. He was happy with David. Maybe when she had their very own baby he would be happy with her.

On Sunday morning Owen arrived while Hal was still giving David a swimming lesson in the heated pool on the patio. Karen was forced to greet him alone and it was with some apprehension that she opened the door to him. To her relief his smile for her was warm and his manner even more so as she showed him into the house and explained David's and Hal's preoccupation. He stopped her as she began to lead him out to the patio.

'I'm in no hurry, Karen, and I owe you an apology.'

'Whatever for?' she retorted lightly, embarrassed by the concern in his eyes.

He gave a rueful little smile. 'You know what for, Karen. On the day you and Hal were married I made an accusation which was obviously wrong.'

'It doesn't matter now, Owen.'

'It matters to me,' he replied with such deep sincerity that Karen could not brush it aside.

'I thought you were out to hurt Hal,' he continued purposefully, 'somehow forcing him into a marriage by holding David over his head. But from something he's said since, I've realised that the marriage was of his making. Quite frankly I don't understand either of you, but since you've been together Hal has become more of the son I used to know, and our relationship is back on its old footing. I've got you to thank for that. He's happier now than I've seen him for years, and I can't doubt that it's your doing, Karen.'

Her heart ached with the wish that it was she who had made Hal happy, but a high-pitched peal of childish laughter, accompanied by a huge splash and Hal's deep chuckle of amusement, told the truer story. Her smile held a tinge of irony. 'I think it's David who's softened Hal, Owen. He loves his son very much.' And he doesn't love me, she added sadly to herself.

'Hey, Pop, watch me!' cried David, the moment they walked out on to the patio. He scrambled out of the pool with a helpful shove from Hal and jumped in again, dog-paddling towards his father, who kept moving backwards just one stroke out of reach. Right across the pool he swam, finally grabbing Hal as he backed against the poolside.

Owen and Karen applauded as Hal lifted him out, and David was beside himself with triumph. Hal grinned at Karen and her heart turned over. She wondered if her answering

smile revealed the feeling which was gradually
consuming her.

'Why don't you get changed and come in
with us, Karen?' Hal invited warmly. 'You
won't mind sitting on the sideline for a while,
will you, Dad?'

'Not if I can watch a beautiful woman in a
bikini,' Owen replied with a teasing twinkle in
his eyes.

Karen quickly demurred, excusing herself by
saying she had to keep an eye on the lunch she
was cooking. A bikini bared too much of her
body and she did not want Hal to notice
anything different about her. She was all too
conscious of the slight thickening of her
waistline and the heightened sensitivity of her
breasts.

The Sunday luncheon was a happy meal,
with Hal being particularly charming to Karen
in front of his father, and David tickled pink to
be the centre of Pop's attention. Afterwards,
while David had an afternoon nap, Owen and
Hal discussed some media issues which were
concerning them, and it was obvious that they
were once more in tune with each other. When
Owen finally suggested taking his leave, Hal
went upstairs to see if David was awake, and it
was then that Owen dropped his bombshell.

'Is there something you should be telling me,
Karen?' he asked with a knowing little smile.

She shrugged, denying any unease at the
question. 'I don't know what you mean.'

He shook his head indulgently at her. 'There's a time in a woman's life, no matter how beautiful she is, when she's positively radiant. Her skin glows with health and vitality, her eyes are brilliant, and her hair gleams. I'm old and my eyes may be tired, but if my memory isn't defective, you give me that impression now. Have you told Hal?'

There was no mistaking his meaning, and Karen flushed to the roots of her gleaming hair. 'It . . . it hasn't been confirmed. I haven't been to a doctor yet.'

'You haven't told him. Well, go to a doctor, my dear, and don't delay about it. There's no more wonderful news in the world, but it will remain our little secret until Hal gives me the word.'

Karen quelled the rise of panic and spoke with quiet insistence. 'You must let me do it my way, Owen.'

His expression of indulgence turned to puzzlement. He sighed and shook his head. 'You play a deep hand, Karen, but rest assured I won't interfere. God knows you've performed miracles in the last few weeks.'

Relief surged through her and she gave him a grateful smile. 'If I ever need advice on a takeover, I'll come to you, Owen.'

He chuckled. 'My dear, I suspect you're the expert, not me.'

She was no expert on anything, especially not on Hal, Karen thought despondently. Don't delay, Owen had advised, and the advice kept taunting her conscience long after Owen had gone. Hal had the right to know that she was pregnant, and it troubled her that she had not told him, but she could not forget his words to her that first afternoon.

He had declared then that he would not leave her alone until she became pregnant. What if he did leave her alone once he knew she was carrying his child? Karen no longer wanted him to leave her alone. It had only been at the first signs of pregnancy that she had finally acknowledged to herself that she loved Hal, deeply and irrevocably. She was afraid to risk any change to their present relationship now. However frustrated she felt with its limitations, it was better than anything she had ever had before.

The problem preyed on her mind over the next few days. She finally decided that it was wrong to keep her pregnancy a secret from him. That was what Kirsty had done, and he would feel cheated again if she did not tell him now, at the outset. Having screwed up her courage, Karen felt hopelessly dampened when Hal came home from work in a black mood.

It had happened twice before, and Karen instantly recognised the signs; the shuttered expression, the dark, brooding stillness of his eyes, the withdrawn manner that not even David could pierce. Any response to his son was reluctant and short, carrying a pained patience that discouraged further attempts at communication. He virtually ignored Karen, making her shrink inside herself.

She did not know what private demons he nursed during these times, whether they were related to his work, or her, or David, or the past. It worried her that Kirsty might not have married Hal because she had known him too well, and knew that marriage did not suit him. Perhaps he was chafing at the restrictions it imposed and he wanted the freedom that he had had with her sister. The seeds of doubt took away all Karen's happiness in the good times they had shared.

The black mood persisted long after David had been put to bed. Dinner was eaten in silence. Karen despaired of ever understanding Hal. He was her husband and he exerted a charismatic influence over her life, yet he was still very much an enigma to her. The need to reach out to him and break the barriers between them grew stronger by the minute. She searched her mind for some line to take, but all she could think of was the baby. Surely he would be pleased by that news. He loved David, and he had said he wanted children.

'Hal . . .'

He had been brooding over his cup of coffee and when he raised his head and met her look of appeal, the expression in the grey eyes choked the words in her throat. Reproach, hatred, anger, bitterness . . . all that was hostile and negative glared back at her. A flicker of guilt shadowed the intense emotion just before he dropped his gaze again.

'What is it?' he muttered uninterestedly.

'It . . . it doesn't matter,' Karen said faintly, too shattered by that one look to say what she had planned. Tomorrow, or the next day, or the next, but not now, she thought despairingly.

Hal did not press her. He sat on, sunk in his own black reverie, not even seeming to notice when Karen cleared the table. Nor did he give any sign that he heard her when Karen said goodnight to him some time later. She went to bed alone and lay in the darkness, fretting over the future. She wanted Hal to be happy with her, but she did not know how to go about achieving that.

She was still awake when he came upstairs. He joined her in bed without a word, but made no move to touch her. Chilled by the terrible sense of separation, Karen reached out a hand and tentatively stroked his arm. It was as if she had activated a switch that released uncontrollable passion.

The next instant Hal was turning to her, taking her with a rough urgency that demanded a total surrender from her. Karen instinctively responded with a fierce need of her own, a need to grab him back from the dark demons which were possessing him. In a silence which was only broken by tortured gasps, they claimed one another in the most primeval act of all, and

when satisfaction had been taken, they lay
exhausted in each other's arms.

Their physical closeness soothed Karen into
sleep, but when she awoke the next morning
Hal was not beside her. He was sitting slumped
in a chair by the glass doors, his gaze seemingly
fixed on the view, and even in profile his face
looked drawn and haggard as if he had not slept
at all. Karen's heart was squeezed by the
loneliness that emanated from him. She threw
off the bedclothes and padded quickly across
the carpet, the closeness of their embrace last
night still pulsing in her memory. She wanted to
recapture that closeness even if it was only
physical.

She slid her hands over his shoulders and
down his chest as she leaned her cheek on his
head. 'What is it, Hal?' she appealed softly.
'Can't you trust me with your confidence?'

He gave a mirthless laugh and flung her
hands off him. In a harsh rejection of her caring
gesture he jerked his head away and stood up.
'Trust you!' he shot at her derisively. 'Do you
take me for a complete fool, Karen?'

She shook her head in hurt bewilderment.
'Why do you say that? What have I done
wrong?'

Again came that mirthless laugh and the
savage mockery was back in his eyes. 'Oh,
you've done nothing wrong, Karen. It's almost
a faultless performance. You've even got my
father believing in it and normally he's a very

astute man, not easily taken in.'

Karen raised her hands in helpless frustration. 'I don't know what you're talking about.'

Hal swung around and caught her arms, shaking her as he grated out his accusation. 'Don't give me that! You're a damned good actress, but I know the facts, remember?'

'Actress?' she repeated dazedly.

His mouth curled into a snarl of contempt. 'For the last six weeks you deserve an Academy Award. Every appearance of being happy, contented, serene with your lot. You even give the impression of a woman in love. Sometimes it even fools me!'

'But I do . . .' She couldn't say it. He wasn't going to believe that she loved him and she could not bear to hear him deride the claim. 'I do care for you, Hal,' she said defeatedly.

His fingers dug into the soft flesh of her arms and his mouth tightened into a grim line. 'Don't lie to me! You're married to a man you don't like, forced to share a son you don't want to share, and you're playing a waiting game. I know it. So when are you going to put the knife in, Karen? What moment are you going to pick to get your revenge on me?'

'I don't want to hurt you!' she cried vehemently, more shaken by his words than by his hands. Her eyes desperately tried to reinforce the truth of what she was saying. 'I want you to be happy, I want to be happy with you. Please believe me, Hal.'

Rejection was written in every taut line of his face as he let her go and paced away from her. 'So what put you in this happy frame of mind, Karen?' he demanded sarcastically. 'The car? The house and servants? Did you decide the easy life was worth having?'

His words hit her like blows, and she recoiled from him, trying and failing to absorb the venom he had fired at her. Her heart writhed over the knowledge that he thought her so mercenary. Her eyes bleakly registered his unrelenting stance, the hard pride of the man. The hopelessness of trying to convince him he was wrong beat through her mind. The barrier he had built between them was impenetrable. Her only weapon was the truth, if only he had ears to hear it. 'I'd live anywhere with you, Hal,' she said quietly.

'Don't take me for a fool!' he retorted bitterly, and his mouth twisted into a sneer. 'I've heard that before, from Kirsty. You and your sister are two of a kind. Neither of you have any regard for the truth. We both know how deeply Kirsty cared for me, don't we, Karen?'

Anger rolled over the hurt. He had no cause to revile either her or Kirsty any more. Restoration had been made for the wrong that had been done. The debt had been paid, with interest. Karen's hand moved to her stomach in an instinctive need to protect the life within . . . the life he had put there out of revenge for the past . . . and her voice throbbed with her own turbulent emotion. 'Kirsty loved you—she loved you with her dying breath. I know it.'

'How could you possibly know such a thing?' he mocked.

'There were things about Kirsty I knew which never had to be put into words.'

Cutting cynicism challenged her. 'Give me one example of something you knew for a positive fact, which was never put into words.'

Somehow she had to prove it to him. She had to make him believe that she was speaking the truth. Any hope of a happy future for their marriage was hanging in the balance right now. Desperation forced Karen to search her mind for the one most telling fact which might turn him around. She found it, and spoke with all the aching urgency in her heart. 'When Kirsty died, she died in terrible agony. I felt it—it woke me up. You know that's true, Hal. You were with her. No one has told me that, but I know it to be a fact.'

His eyes swept her with contempt. 'You're wrong, Karen. That wasn't even a good try. Kirsty didn't die in agony. She had hardly any pain at all. I'll tell you precisely how she died, because you obviously don't know. She had one wound, only one, but it severed her femoral artery and nothing could stop the bleeding. She was in shock, but if there was any pain, it was minimal.'

The blood drained from Karen's face. A

wave of dizziness made her feel faint. What Hal said couldn't be true—it couldn't! She had felt Kirsty's pain, so strong it had been that it had pierced her heart from halfway around the world. Slowly understanding dawned, understanding of what Kirsty had been suffering in those fatal few minutes.

'So you've deluded yourself over this, Karen,' Hal jeered at her relentlessly. 'But I don't intend to delude myself over you.'

He was beyond reaching; it was hopeless even trying. A wave of nausea kept her silent for a moment, but the attack on her integrity had to be answered. Pride dictated it, and the emotional wounds he had so brutally inflicted cried out for some redress.

'I once called you a monster, and I was right!' she cried. 'All you're concerned with is yourself. You think you know everything, but you're so blind, Hal Chissolm, you wouldn't know love if you stumbled over it!'

Her passionate words did not move him one iota. He stared back at her with cold, unyielding eyes, eyes which had passed the most heinous judgement on her and her sister. But Karen wasn't finished. She was going to hammer the truth home to him if it was the last thing she ever did.

'I didn't say Kirsty died in physical pain, Hal. She died in terrible agony, an agony of heart and mind you've never known. But I've known it. I felt it with her, and it was far, far worse than any physical pain, almost unendurable. She loved you. She knew she was dying, that she was losing you for ever. She had promised me you'd never know about David, but she couldn't bear not to tell you. It was the only way that some part of her could keep hold of you. That's how deeply she loved you, Hal. She would have done anything for you, even to betraying me. You can choose not to believe me, but that is the truth.'

His face slowly turned ashen. 'Oh, my God!' It was an appalled whisper. His hand lifted and rubbed at his eyes. When it dropped away he looked at Karen with searing torment. 'No . . . she couldn't have meant that. It couldn't have been like that . . .'

'Oh, yes, it was!' Karen hurled back at him, as relentless as he had been.

He shook his head and moved blindly in his perturbation, half staggering against the wall. 'You don't understand. She said . . .' He looked back at Karen, his eyes glazed with shock. 'What have I done?' The words were more a self-castigation than a question, but Karen had an answer for him. It burst from the pain of his rejection of her and everything she had done in her love for him. 'I'll tell you what you've done. You've made me pregnant! I'm carrying your child, Hal, so you don't have to nerve yourself up to taking Kirsty's sister any more. You've succeeded in what you set out to do. It's done. Are you satisfied now?'

'No, Karen, it's not like that. You've got to listen. There's something I have to tell you.' He plunged back across the room towards her, hands outstretched in appeal.

'I've heard enough!' she said bitterly, and hit his hands away. Tears gushed into her eyes. 'Leave me alone! You don't care! It's all been revenge to you, hasn't it? Even to . . . to . . . oh, you are a monster! Just leave me alone. You've got what you wanted!' she wailed in uncontrollable distress, and ran into the *ensuite* bathroom.

She locked herself in and cried her heart out. She knew the truth of what he thought of her now and it clawed through her mind again and again, shredding every illusion of a happy life with him. All this time he had seen her as a scheming actress, not a woman who had come to love him. And she had given herself to him so unreservedly. It was so shaming, the way she had laid herself bare for him to whip with his scathing cynicism. No more, she vowed with all the strength of her hurt. No more would she be a whipping boy for Hal Chissolm. He didn't want her love and she would never show it again. Never.

She was running late by the time she pulled herself together and got ready for work. Hal had left her alone. David was not in his bedroom and his discarded pyjamas indicated that he was dressed. Karen found both husband and son in the breakfast room, seated at the table. David's cereal bowl was empty, which meant he had eaten. Karen ignored Hal, just as he had ignored her at the table last night. She did not even walk into the room but spoke from the doorway.

'Come on, David, it's time to leave. Say goodbye to your father,' she ordered peremptorily.

Her stern voice startled him into obeying her immediately, and barely a minute later they were both out of the house. She turned him away from the path to the garages and hurried him out to the street, heading for the nearest bus stop.

David tugged at her hand protestingly. 'Why aren't we going in the car?'

'Because we're catching the bus from now on,' she replied in a tone which brooked no questions.

They had been standing at the bus stop for several minutes when Hal's BMW pulled up beside them. He alighted, rounded the bonnet in a few quick strides, opened the passenger door and met Karen's defiant pride with steely determination. 'Get in,' he commanded.

Before Karen could stop David he had slid his hand out of her hold and scrambled into the car. With her purpose already half defeated and conscious of the other people at the bus stop watching them curiously, Karen decided this was no place for a scene. She took the passenger seat and Hal slammed the door shut on her.

She sat staring straight ahead, stubbornly silent as he drove to the kindergarten. Hal did not speak either, and for once David had nothing to say. The atmosphere in the car was thick enough to daunt even a child, Karen thought angrily. Well, whatever Hal thought he was doing she certainly had an answer ready for him! On their arrival at the kindergarten, he held Karen's wrist tightly and told David to go inside. As soon as David was out of earshot she turned fiercely on Hal.

'Let go of me this instant! You've violated my body for the last time, Hal Chissolm. Touch me again and I'll head straight for the divorce court! I've got a better custody case now, haven't I?'

Bleak, expressionless eyes looked back at her. 'What's wrong with the Porsche?'

'I don't want your fancy car! Nor do I give a damn for your fancy house and servants. I managed perfectly well in my own little home. And you can keep your money—I supported myself and David long before you came along and I can do it again!'

Hal turned his head aside as pain spasmed across his face. He drew a deep breath and spoke haltingly, as if each word hurt him. 'Karen ... when I married you ... I made myself responsible for your support. And David's. And any children we might have. Work if you please, but don't ... don't overtax yourself when there's no need. Anything that I own is yours, without strings. I'll move to another bedroom tonight.' He pulled the car keys out of the ignition and pressed them into her hand. 'Use this car to get home. I'll hire a taxi.'

Before she could form any reply at all, he was out of the car and striding towards the telephone box on the corner. For a few moments Karen sat completely still. It was the end of their marriage. No matter that it had all been a farce anyway, she felt bereft, cold, empty.

Until she remembered the baby. Her hand moved slowly over her stomach. Somewhere inside there a baby was growing. Her baby, and Hal's. She blinked back tears and got out of the car. Life went on.

CHAPTER TEN

LIFE went on, but to Karen it was utterly miserable. Her pregnancy was confirmed by her doctor, but there was no joy in it for her. No joy at home either. True to his word, Hal had moved out of their bedroom suite and Karen hated the loneliness of the huge king-size bed. No matter that she told herself that he had only been using her, she missed his warm embrace in the dark hours of the night.

And Hal changed. He became silent and more reserved, even with David. His manner to Karen remained kind and considerate, but there was no sparkle of happiness in him. Gone were the moments of pleasure they had shared during the first six weeks of their marriage. He was still very loving to David, but in a quiet way, and when Karen was on the scene he deflected much of David's attention to her. But David could not fill the void that the separation from Hal had created. Even though the situation was mostly of her own making, Karen felt strangely deserted.

Most nights she cried herself to sleep, and the days were a struggle to get through. Morning sickness became a daily occurrence. She kept a careful diet, but she seemed to be putting on too much weight. She felt gross and unattractive, which depressed her further. She had known other women whose pregnancy had not shown for five or six months, but obviously that was not going to be the case with her. The doctor explained that some women carried more fluid than others and there was no reason for her to be disturbed about it. She was doing just fine.

But she wasn't doing fine. Apart from the morning sickness she felt tired all the time and tears gushed into her eyes at any little mishap. One night she dropped a cup in the kitchen, and she was kneeling over the pieces on the floor, in uncontrollable floods of tears, when Hal came in. She felt too weak to resist his hold on her as he lifted her up and drew her into a comforting embrace. She just laid her head on his shoulder and sobbed.

'Karen, you can't go on like this,' he said quietly, his voice full of concern. 'You must give up work. You're not having enough rest. I'll take David to the kindergarten every day if you want him to continue there.'

It sounded like concern for her. He was stroking her hair as if he cared. But it couldn't be so, she thought miserably. He was only worried about the baby. His baby. She dragged her head up and pushed away from him. He seemed reluctant to let her go, but he did.

'All right,' she sniffed, 'I'll give up work.' She took a deep, steadying breath. 'I think David needs the company of other children, so I'll arrange that he keep on at the kindergarten two days a week. That shouldn't disturb your schedule too much.'

His eyes reproached her. 'David is my son too, Karen. I don't mind going out of my way for him. Every day, if that's what you think he should have.' She shook her head. 'Not without me there.' Then knowing she had unwittingly hurt him, she added more softly, 'I'm sorry, Hal, I didn't mean you wouldn't care to do it for him. I know you care.'

'For you too, Karen, if only you'd let me.'

He looked sincere. He sounded sincere. But it had to be for the baby; he didn't really mean her. 'I'll . . . I'll be all right,' she stammered defensively, and turned away, hurrying out of the room before her need for him could tempt her back into his arms.

Hal didn't follow her. Not that Karen had expected him to, but she felt more lonely than ever. Despite his opinion of her she still loved him, could not help loving him. And that was another burden she had to bear on her own.

Another month passed. Karen was beginning to feel grotesque, her body was so swollen. The doctor also showed concern when she went for her monthly check-up. He examined her with more thoroughness than usual, frowning and double-checking. Fear chased around her mind.

'Is there something wrong?' she asked anxiously. The morning sickness had finally passed. Was that a good sign or a bad sign? she worried frantically.

'No, not at all,' the doctor assured her. 'However, I'd just like a further check, so I'll make an appointment for you to have an ultra-sound scan. And I'll also get you to see a specialist obstetrician.'

'Why?' Karen demanded, panicking at the measures being taken.

'Nothing to worry about, Mrs Chissolm. We send most pregnant mothers to have a scan at about this time—standard procedure. You can even be told your baby's sex if you want to know.'

'But the obstetrician?'

'I'm sure your husband would want you to have the best of care, Mrs Chissolm.' He gave a cheerful grin. 'Husbands can get more uptight than their wives over having babies! Now I'll just get my nurse to make the appointments for you.'

Karen fretted all the way home. There was something wrong. The doctor wasn't telling her, but there was surely something wrong. She was in such a state of emotional tension when Hal came home that she burst into tears as soon as she saw him.

'It's not my fault, Hal,' she sobbed into his chest. 'I didn't do anything wrong—I swear it!'

'Hush now,' he murmured, gently hugging her closer.

'I did everything the doctor told me, truly I

did!' she cried hysterically.

'Karen, don't take on so. Just tell me why you're so upset.'

Under his comforting touch she spilled out everything that had happened in the doctor's office. Hal soothed her fears with a calm stream of common sense, then walked her upstairs and put her to bed, insisting that he would look after dinner. He brought her a meal on a tray, stayed with her while she ate some of it, saw to David's needs until his bedtime, then returned to Karen.

'Hal, I really have taken care of myself,' she assured him, still racked with anxiety. 'It's my baby too.'

He sat down on the bed next to her and took one fretful hand in his, calming it with his warmth. 'It's our baby, Karen, and I know you want it as much as I do. Don't keep upsetting yourself. The doctor didn't say there was anything wrong.'

'But . . .'

'He was quite right—I do want the best of care for you, and I'm coming with you to both of those appointments.'

Tears flooded into her eyes again. 'Thank you,' she whispered huskily, wishing he was holding more of her than her hand. Her need for him was so great at that moment that pride and hurt were crushed under its weight. 'Hal . . . would you stay with me tonight? I . . . I don't want to be alone.'

Her eyes were too blurred to see his expression clearly, but it seemed to be a reflection of what she felt. 'I don't want to be alone either,' he murmured, and gathered her up into a tender embrace. His mouth brushed over her hair again and again, planting whispers of kisses which seemed to express the same yearning that was in Karen's soul. She clung unashamedly to him, revelling in his tenderness and his strength, breathing in the warm, male scent of him, wanting him never to let her go.

He stayed with her all night, and Karen could once more dream that he loved her. He did not make love to her, but he held her in his arms, cradling her with a tenderness which was more moving than any sexual overture. She did not care if it was only compassion that kept him with her. They were together again. Neither of them spoke a word about the issue, but Hal did not return to his separate bedroom the next night, or the next, or any night before Karen's appointment for the ultra-sound scan.

She had been instructed to drink two pints of water before going to the medical centre; her bladder had to be full for the scan to be successful. Karen forced the water down, but she felt dreadfully uncomfortable on the trip to the centre. She doubted that she would have made it without Hal. It distressed her when a young girl technician separated them.

'How long will this take?' demanded Hal, as tense and anxious as herself.

'About half an hour, Mr Chissolm,' the technician answered cheerily.

Just routine work for her, Karen thought grimly as she was led away. She was placed on a table and a machine was suspended over her. The technician rubbed an oil over her stomach and then ran some small gadget over it.

'This won't hurt, Mrs Chissolm,' the girl assured her. 'I'm going to take a picture of your baby—the very first picture. You'll be able to start your photograph album today!'

Karen could not respond to the girl's smile. The minutes ticked by. The girl chattered on for a few minutes, then her small talk dwindled off and she frowned with concentration. 'Sorry to keep you, Mrs Chissolm. I'm having trouble with the angles, getting a clear image. Won't be long now.'

'What's wrong?' Karen cried in panic.

'Nothing wrong, Mrs Chissolm. Just a question of angles.'

It was nearly an hour before the technician was satisfied. 'You said I could have a picture of my baby,' Karen reminded her, every instinct screaming for a confirmation that nothing was wrong.

'I'm sorry, Mrs Chissolm, but I'll have to leave that up to your obstetrician. That's standard procedure in these cases,' she said sweetly.

Karen could not speak again. She felt sick and faint. The girl led her back to Hal, and

Karen heard him questioning the girl. His voice held a strident tone, but the young technician could not be moved from her stance.

'It's not my position to comment, Mr Chissolm. You have to see your wife's obstetrician.'

The next few days were absolute anguish. Hal tried to ease Karen's fears, but she sensed that he shared them. Owen came charging around to see her.

'Karen, there's a man at Sydney University who's the leader of his field. If you don't get satisfaction from this Dr Grayson you're going to see, I'll get Professor Bellamy to sort it out. He's the man. Don't you worry.'

But Owen was worried. Karen thanked him for his concern, but she had the terrible feeling that whatever was happening inside her body was irrevocable. Without Hal's reassuring support she could not have kept going in any sensible fashion. He was so good to her that she sometimes fantasised that he really did love her. Even on the morning of her appointment with the obstetrician, Hal cajoled her into a light breakfast and a large glass of milk, saying it was good for the baby and everything was going to be all right.

But she could feel his tension as he drove her to Macquarie Street where all the top specialists resided. It was an early appointment, nine-thirty in the morning, and there were no other patients in the waiting-room of Dr Grayson's offices. Hal held her paused in the doorway and spoke with a low urgency that touched her deeply.

'Karen, no matter what happens, this is our baby. And we'll love it.'

How could she have ever called him a monster? Karen wondered, loving him fiercely in that anguished moment of sharing. He was a good man, a good, loving man whom she was proud to have as her husband.

A white-uniformed woman rose from behind a desk and ushered them into the consulting room. Dr Grayson was a tall, thin, distinguished-looking man, somewhere in his fifties, and he beamed delight at them through his gold-rimmed spectacles. His wide smile eased a little of Karen's tension. Surely a doctor of any sensitivity would not be smiling if he had bad news for them.

'Mr and Mrs Chissolm, it's a great pleasure to meet you,' he boomed, taking Hal's hand and shaking it vigorously.

Karen felt faint. She sank into the nearest chair as the doctor turned to her. 'Is that chair comfortable enough for you, Mrs Chissolm? We'll have to be taking the greatest care of you now.'

'It's fine, thank you,' she croaked.

Dr Grayson rubbed his hands together gleefully. 'Well, before we go any further, I'd like your permission to invite one of my colleagues to join this meeting. His name is

Professor Martin Bellamy, and he's one of the top four or five obstetricians in Australia. In his specialty he's regarded as a world expert.'

'Why do we need him?' Hal demanded curtly.

'I'd like him to tell you that himself,' Dr Grayson replied, still beaming delight.

'As you wish,' conceded Hal, exchanging anxious looks with Karen.

The doctor opened a side-door and called in a man who was somewhat older than himself but who carried an air of immense authority, despite his high-domed bald head. He also exuded a barely suppressed excitement as he was introduced to Hal and Karen. He took a chair to the side of the doctor's desk. Hal and Dr Grayson sat down.

'If I could start, Professor?' the doctor demurred indulgently.

'By all means,' was the eager reply.

'Mr and Mrs Chissolm, you are going to be the parents of twins.'

Is that all? Karen thought dazedly. Just twins? She glanced at Hal to see his reaction.

His jaw tightened. 'And what's the bad news?' he demanded.

The doctor gave a rueful smile. 'Well, the umbilical cord of one of the twins is caught around the neck of the other, but . . .'

'If I might interrupt,' Professor Bellamy put in, 'there's nothing to be alarmed about, Mr Chissolm. This has happened before. We've handled births like that many, many times, and never lost a baby. The finest medical team in Australia has already volunteered, free of charge, to be at the birth of your twins, because we suspect—only suspect, mind you—that you're in the process of making medical history.'

'What are you talking about?' Hal fired at him irritably. 'What the devil is going on?'

The mention of the medical team had upset Karen too. Precisely what medical history was going to be made? Owen had told her that Professor Bellamy was the leader in his field.

The Professor smiled reassurance. 'I shall explain—just a moment of your patience, Mr Chissolm. You may or may not be aware that there are different types of twins. Most sets are what we call fraternal twins, who come from two different eggs which happen to have been fertilised at the same time. Then we have identical twins, which are not so common. Such twins are born from a single egg that separated into two parts early in its development, and each part becomes one of the twins. Sometimes, and it's very rare, that separation of the egg does not occur until the egg has begun to develop right and left-handed characteristics.'

He paused, his forehead puckered into a frown. 'If separation occurs too late, we get Siamese twins. The timing is critical, a matter of a few days. However, if the egg has separated just prior to this critical period, we get a case of mirror-image identical twins.'

He breathed a sigh of satisfaction before continuing. 'I'm recognised as a world expert on mirror-image identical twins, yet in over forty years of specialisation I've only seen two cases, the last over twenty years ago. The babies your wife is carrying could very well be such a case. We're not sure, but from the ultrasound scan there's every indication that it is so; and if they are mirror-image identical twins, Mr Chissolm, both you and your wife need to be psychologically prepared.'

Karen breathed a silent prayer of thanks. That was all it was! Something they didn't understand and wanted to know. Something she already knew. The loneliness she had felt from the loss of Kirsty was somehow appeased with the knowledge that a cycle was being reborn.

'You'll have to explain that too, Professor,' urged Hal. 'What's the difficulty about these twins?'

The Professor had the air of climbing on to his hobby-horse. 'There'll be certain basic differences between the two. One will be right-handed, the other left-handed. Their personalities will complement each other, one extrovert, one introvert. Together they form one single unit and will operate as such. They will understand one another better than any other two human beings.'

'So?' prompted Hal, not seeing any great problem.

The Professor smiled. 'I'll go back to my last case. From the moment of their birth, these children had very specific requirements. If you placed one child on the wrong side of the other, they were extremely distressed. The left-handed child has to be laid on the correct side of the right-handed child. They're in actuality two halves of one entity and when they're placed correctly one can observe it in their physical contact, a oneness which is unique. Every doctor and nurse in the country will want to see it.'

'No! The birth of our children will not be turned into a circus!' Hal burst out, fiercely protective.

Karen leaned over and pressed his hand reassuringly. 'It's all right, Hal. It won't hurt them and it's something we should give, so that others can understand.'

'Thank you, Mrs Chissolm,' the Professor jumped in quickly. 'I cannot stress too much that if what we suspect eventuates, and your twins are mirror-imaged, you must be prepared psychologically. They will act as one unit. There's every reason to believe that such twins can sometimes be telepathic with each other.'

'Good God!' Hal was aghast.

Karen could barely suppress a smile.

'I'm afraid so, Mr Chissolm,' the Professor insisted. 'I'll give you a few examples. At one time we separated one set of these twins and offered one a chocolate biscuit. She ate it and the other twin knew nothing about it. We offered her two chocolate biscuits and the other twin immediately came running. The twin with the biscuits had communicated with the other telepathically, letting her know there was a biscuit for her.'

Karen giggled over the memory.

Hal frowned at her. 'It could have been coincidence,' he argued.

'There were too many such coincidences, Mr Chissolm. And one of the most telling examples ... the twins sat for a maths test. They were seated at opposite ends of the room. In every prior test they had the same questions right and the same questions wrong. No deviation whatsoever. But this time one received a higher mark than the other. It resulted in the only known time in their lives that the twins fought—after the test one tore into the other. When they were finally separated and calmed down, one accused the other of shutting her out, refusing to give her an answer in the test.'

'Kirsty wanted to come first,' muttered Karen, recalling the hurt she had felt.

'What?'

Karen turned a wry smile to the Professor. 'I'd given Kirsty the answer to the previous question, but she shut me out on the next one and beat me by one mark. We were seven at the time. You've been talking about my sister and myself, Professor.'

His mouth dropped open. 'My God! Then you must be Karen Balfour! Do you realise that you and your sister were my last case of mirror-imaged twins in this country? The last ones recognised and documented!'

'You and Kirsty?' Hal gasped beside her.

She turned reluctantly, not wanting to recall the argument she had with Hal over Kirsty, the argument which had laid bare the festering sores of their relationship. Yet she desperately wanted his belief in her. 'I did tell you I knew, Hal, about Kirsty's death,' she said softly. 'As we grew older we shut each other off, but in times of intense stress, we knew. We ... we connected.'

She heaved a sad sigh. 'I know it's difficult for others to understand, that's why Kirsty and I kept it to ourselves. But it's true ... what the Professor says. We were different, yet so close. So very close that she could start a sentence and I could finish it for her exactly.'

Hal was shaking his head, but not in disbelief. His eyes held awe and pain and understanding. 'The wrong mirror,' he murmured, half under his breath. 'So clear to Kirsty, so meaningless to me.'

Karen had no time to question the strange words.

'Extraordinary!' the Professor exclaimed. 'This will certainly make medical history. One

of the Balfour twins! For you, a mirror-image
twin, to give birth to mirror-image twins . . . a
chance in millions. Billions.' He recollected
himself in an abrupt change of manner,
dropping his voice to mournful regret. 'And you
say your sister has died, Mrs Chissolm?'

'Yes. Quite recently,' Hal answered for her.

'That must have been extremely traumatic
for   you,'   the   Professor   murmured
sympathetically.

Karen drew in a deep breath and faced him
again. 'Yes. Yes, it was. I doubt that anyone
else could understand. You surprise me, Professor. I didn't know anyone had compiled a case
history on us,' she added questioningly.

'It was not intended that you know. Your
parents insisted that you were to lead a
completely natural life, and I agreed with them.
It was most important. I advised them on facets
of your upbringing and they reported back to
me, right up until their deaths. After that . . .
well, I honoured the agreement made that you
were never to be bothered with experiments, or
made to feel odd in any way.'

His mouth twisted into an ironic smile. 'I
doubt that I can advise you, Mrs Chissolm. You
know more about such cases than I do. I would
be most grateful if you'd enlighten me on
certain points, particularly about the . . .'

'Not today, Professor,' Hal cut in firmly. 'My
wife has been under great strain this last week,
worrying about the baby. The babies,' he

corrected himself with a feeling sigh. 'Now that we know that everything's all right and under control, I'd like to take her home.'

'Of course,' Professor Bellamy agreed promptly. 'We'll be seeing her again soon. This is tremendously exciting, isn't it, Doctor?'

'It certainly is,' Dr Grayson declared with enthusiasm. 'We'll be wanting you to come here for weekly check-ups, Mrs Chissolm. My nurse will give you a card with your appointments. Do you want to know the sex of the babies?'

Karen looked anxiously at Hal.

'That's up to you,' he said softly.

'I'd rather wait until they're born.'

He nodded and turned back to the doctor. 'There is one point I'd like clarified . . .' He hesitated, then plunged on determinedly, 'Can my wife and I have sexual intercourse without causing a problem to the babies?'

A tide of hot blood flooded up Karen's neck and scorched into her cheeks. She couldn't look at Hal. Did he want her? Did he really want her when she was so lumpy and undesirable?

'You would have to be very careful the last two months. Penetration should not be too deep, but apart from that there's no problem with having sexual intercourse. I would suggest that the safest method is on your side, with you behind your wife.' The Professor turned to Karen with a smile. 'By the way, Mrs Chissolm, do you want a photograph of your babies?'

'Yes, but I think I'd rather wait until after they're born.'

'Then I'll keep it for you.'

Hal thanked him and helped Karen up out of her chair. The two obstetricians fussed around her for a few moments and somehow she managed to mouth polite goodbyes. Finally they were out of the consulting room, out of the building, and safely enclosed in Hal's car. Still Karen could not bring herself to look at Hal. She took a deep breath and screwed up her courage.

'Why did you ask that?'

'Karen ... look at me,' came the quiet command.

She flicked him a look and her eyes were caught by the intensity of emotion in his.

'Are you happy about the twins?' he asked.

'Are you?'

He sighed and a smile tugged at his mouth. 'I told you, I'd love whatever we had. Now answer me.'

'I'm very happy about it.' Just the thought of her twin babies made a smile light up her face until she remembered her own question. 'You haven't answered me, Hal.'

He reached over and took her hand. 'It wasn't just to make you pregnant those first few weeks, Karen. I wanted to make love to you. And you wanted it too. I know I fouled it up and I was wrong. I knew I was wrong that morning we argued about Kirsty, but I'd said too much and hurt you too deeply.'

He dragged in a deep breath and his eyes held an eloquent appeal. 'I really want this marriage of ours to work, Karen. I want to go through this pregnancy with you, be with you as much as possible. But if I stay in your bed, I don't think I can control myself for that long. I want you, Karen. Would you mind very much?'

Hope was thundering through her heart. Her throat was very dry and she could hardly speak. 'You want me? Like this?'

He shook his head at her in incredulity. 'Don't you know you look more beautiful every day?'

'But I don't! I look terrible.'

Hal leaned forward and started the car. 'I think I'll take you home and prove that you don't look terrible!'

And there was no more discussion. Hal took her home and straight up to their bedroom. He undressed her very slowly. It was not dark, and the bright light of noon was streaming into the room. Karen could see the soft reverence in his eyes as they worshipped her swollen body and a lovely warm glow ran through her veins.

Very gently he laid her on the bed, and stripped himself of his clothes. Karen was reminded of the first time when he had stood over her, so tense with masculine aggression, but the only real similarity was his arousal. He was excited by her, and his arousal fired hers even before he began kissing her breasts with exquisite tenderness. She melted under his soft caresses, and when his mouth took hers in sensual plunder, she responded with urgent passion, wanting all of him so much that she completely forgot that her body was cumbersome.

He held her back against him, caressing her into a position that eased his entry so that it almost came as a surprise when she felt him slide inside her. He used a slow rhythm which was unbelievably erotic, and again and again Karen shuddered with pleasure. His arms wrapped her body so closely to his that she could feel his muscles rippling. And his mouth grazed across her hair, her shoulders, her arms, constantly arousing a sensitivity which begged to be satisfied with more and more kisses.

Time was meaningless. She closed her eyes and surrendered herself to him, utterly and completely. She didn't care that he was only giving her physical love. It was enough for now, more than enough. And he wanted their marriage to work. He wanted to stay with her. If it could always be like this, she would not ask for more.

CHAPTER ELEVEN

THE pregnancy wore Karen down. Although Hal was attentive and solicitous, she could not help feeling it was only for the babies' sake. He never spoke of love—not love for her. She grew bigger with child. Hal was fascinated with her body. Every night he made a sensual ceremony of rubbing oil over her stomach, soothing the tight, stretched skin, and if he felt the babies move, his eyes would sparkle with delight. His children, Karen thought with increasing despondency.

And at other times she wondered how Kirsty could have been so wrong about Hal. There was no doubt in Karen's mind now that he would have welcomed her sister's pregnancy. Kirsty had loved Hal; she must have known he would love a child. Why had she hidden David from him? Kirsty had never been cruel—selfish maybe, but never cruel. She had wanted to be first, needed to be first. Perhaps she had thought the child would come first with Hal, and she couldn't bear to be second in his affections.

Karen could understand that. There were times that she felt insanely jealous of the children she carried inside her. She desperately

wanted Hal to shower his love on her in the
same proportions as she wanted to shower her
love on him. Only the intimacy he shared with
her in the dark hours of the night gave her some
outlet to her stifled emotions. And she was even
deprived of that in the last couple of months of
her pregnancy; Hal was too concerned about
the babies' safety to risk sexual intercourse.

Those last two months were terrible. She
grew huge. It was exhausting to go for short
walks, let alone do the pre-natal exercises that
Dr Grayson had advised. She felt cut off from
Hal, cut off from playing with David, cut off
from everything except her own grotesque
physical self. She was totally miserable and
longed for the pregnancy to be over.

When it was still two weeks short of her full
term, Dr Grayson suggested she be admitted to
hospital. But Karen refused. As lonely and
depressed as she felt at home, it was better to be
there with Hal and David than in some
impersonal hospital room, waiting to be visited. Hal tried to persuade her into going to
hospital, but she burst into tears, convinced
that he didn't want her any more, that only the
babies mattered to him. Hal quickly back-
tracked, saying she could do as she wished, but
he was clearly worried.

Karen's back ached, but she said nothing,
not wanting to suffer Hal's concern. Every time
he frowned at her she wanted to cry. The first
bad pain came three days after Dr Grayson's

suggestion. She and Hal had just finished dinner and she bit her lip to stifle a little moan of agony.

'Anything wrong?' asked Hal, anxiety sharpening his tone.

'No. Just uncomfortable,' she half-lied.

They went to bed. Karen lay awake, waiting, watching the clock. Another pain sliced through her body. It came almost an hour after the first. The next one surprised her forty minutes later. Then thirty-five ... thirty ... thirty ... thirty ... regular contractions. By two o'clock in the morning she no longer had any doubt about what was happening. She woke Hal.

Almost instantly he was up on his elbow. 'What is it?'

'I think we'd better go to the hospital.'

'Contractions?'

'Coming regularly. Every half hour.'

'Hell! You should have woken me before!' He was out of bed and scrabbling with the telephone in a panicky rush.

'I wasn't sure at first,' she answered him calmly. 'There's plenty of time, Hal.'

'We're not taking any chances on that, Karen.'

No ... no chances on anything bad happening to the babies, Karen thought grimly, then berated herself for the thought. She wanted them born safe and soundly too. Hal's concern was only natural. Having alerted Dr Grayson that she was in labour, he was a whirlwind of activity; pulling clothes on, getting David up and dressed, hushing the little boy's excitement, helping Karen into a dressing-gown and half carrying her down the stairs.

Another contraction hit her during the drive into the hospital, and so sharp was the pain that she cried out. Hal instantly braked the car and pulled over to the side of the road. 'Go on,' she gasped, trying to employ the breathing exercises she had practised.

'Karen . . .'

'Go on,' she insisted. 'It's all right.'

He drove at maniacal speed, casting anxious glances at her all the way. David was unnaturally quiet—probably frightened, Karen thought fleetingly, but she had to concentrate on her breathing now. Do it right. Do everything right. She had come a long way and the time was almost over. She had to satisfy Hal, make him happy.

He was relieved to hand her over to the professionals at the hospital, waiting only for the assurance that Dr Grayson and Professor Bellamy had been told of Karen's arrival at the hospital before he left with David. Hal promised he would be back as soon as he had taken David to Owen, but Karen felt deserted and terribly alone, watching him stride away from her.

She was wheeled into a preparation room. White-uniformed people flocked around her, but she felt alienated from them. They were normal, going about their everyday business. She was locked into a world of rhythmic pain which they didn't share. She meant nothing to these people; they were only interested in the miracle that her body was about to produce.

She was moved to another room. A clock hung on the wall above the end of her bed, an old-fashioned clock that ticked, and Karen watched it as if her life depended on it. The minute hand crawled around, measuring her contractions as fifteen minutes apart. Ten minutes. It seemed an interminable age before Hal returned.

An intense wave of gratitude washed through her. She would not be alone any more. Hal had shared her pregnancy as intimately as any person could, and she needed him to be with her. He took the chair by her bed and held her hand.

'Is there anything I can do for you, Karen?' he asked softly.

'Just stay . . .' Another pain sliced through her and a tortured groan broke from her throat. She bent forward, trying to ride with it, and her hand gripped Hal's with knuckle-white intensity until the contraction receded. 'Stay with me. Please!' she gasped, her eyes begging for his patience.

'My God!' His face was white. 'How long does this go on for?'

'I don't know. Please, Hal . . .'

'Of course I'll stay with you. Do you think I'd let you go through this by yourself?'

'Thank you,' she whispered.

He shook his head and there was pain in his eyes when he spoke. 'Do you still think I'm a callous monster, Karen?'

'No . . . no . . .'

He heaved a sigh of relief, but the pain in his eyes seemed to deepen. 'I wish . . .' Again he shook his head. 'I seem to have done everything wrong with you. And now there's nothing I can do. I feel so damned useless.'

'Not useless. I . . . I need you.' I love you, I love you, her heart cried, but she could not lay that burden on him. He was feeling guilty. She understood that it was not easy for him to witness her pain. He had wanted her pregnant, made her pregnant, only ever anticipating the end result, not the ordeal of labour that brought it about. Karen had sat through it with Kirsty, yet the memory in no way compared to what she was suffering now.

Hal was telling her when to breathe, calming her, wiping her forehead. She was barely aware of Dr Grayson and Professor Bellamy as they examined her.

'Can't you give her something?' Hal burst out, strained beyond endurance. 'She can't go on like this! It's not right!'

'I can give your wife an epidural injection, Mr Chissolm,' Dr Grayson answered calmly, 'but you must understand it will relax her and slow down the labour.'

'If it gives her relief . . .'

'No . . . no . . .' Karen cut in urgently. 'Don't want . . . slowing down. Might hurt babies.'

'To hell with the babies!' Hal grated fiercely. 'You're not going through any more of this, Karen. You matter more to me than any children ever could!'

The words thudded into her mind, echoing, echoing, gathering a power that made the pain meaningless. She mattered to him, more than the babies! It wasn't just guilt. He really did care about her. And she loved him, loved him, loved him. She wanted to give him his children.

'I can bear it. Please . . . let me.'

Anguished grey eyes questioned hers feverishly. 'Are you sure, Karen?'

'Yes.'

He turned to the doctors. 'How much longer?'

'Water breaking now,' the doctor remarked matter-of-factly.

And the pain changed. Where before it had sliced through her, now it dragged at her body. She hung on to Hal, frightened by the tearing length of this new torture.

'I'll never put you through this again, Karen, I swear it,' he muttered grimly.

She couldn't speak. Only her eyes spoke, needing him, needing his love and all that he was, being with her for better, for worse, in sickness or in health, till death . . . ?

'I love you.'

Had she imagined that hoarse whisper? The grey eyes were filmed with tears. She saw his mouth form the words again.

'I love you.'

Soft, beautiful words, words of intense emotion, torn from his heart, wrapping around her, seeping into her soul.

'One big push now, Mrs Chissolm.'

Dr Grayson's voice held an extra edge of excitement, piercing the haze in her mind. Hal's eyes begged for it to be over. She pushed and felt a rush of release. There was a flurry of activity at the other end of the bed. A baby cried. Hal did not look; he was concentrating entirely on her, loving her. And the baby didn't matter. Only the love in Hal's eyes mattered.

He stroked her cheek and leaned over and kissed her forehead. Karen wanted to reach up and pull his mouth down to hers, but another shaft of agony rent her body. Soon . . . it had to be over soon, she thought wildly. Long, pain-ridden moments, but Hal's love sustained her through them. Then again the sensation of release and another baby cried.

Their twins had been born! The wonder of that thought spilled joy on top of joy. Hal loved her and she had given birth to their children. Her throat was impossibly dry, but she croaked out the words. 'What . . . what sex are they?'

'Girls, Mrs Chissolm. Two beautiful, identical, perfectly healthy little girls. And a good size too. No humidi-crib needed for these lusty infants!' the doctor assured her in a tone of triumph.

Girls! Tears swam into Karen's eyes. Hal brushed his lips gently over hers. 'Just like their beautiful mother,' he whispered huskily.

And Kirsty, she thought happily. Kirsty who had given her Hal's child and brought her to him, the one man who was the love of her life. All the miseries of her marriage faded into insignificance. They meant nothing against the incredible wonder of Hal's loving her.

She felt totally exhausted, but it was an exhaustion that held a marvellous fulfilment. She was truly the mother of Hal's children now. The doctors showed them to her—such little babies, but so beautiful. And with Hal's black hair. Karen was too choked with emotion to speak. She was given an injection and drifted into sleep, sublimely at peace with her world.

The scent of roses teased her awake. It was dark, but dim floor-lights lent visibility to the room. She turned her head to look at the roses she knew must be there, but the dark figure sitting by her bed caught her gaze first. He was slumped in the chair, his head dipped forward. He was dozing, and Karen wondered how long he had been sitting beside her. A warm pleasure curled around her heart.

'Hal?' she called softly.

He jerked upright. 'Karen, are you all right? Shall I ring for a nurse?'

She smiled reassurance. 'No, don't ring—I'm fine. Thank you for being here.'

'The babies are fine too. The star attraction of the hospital, one might say,' he added wryly. He stood up and gently sat on her bed. 'Are you really all right, Karen?' he asked with urgent insistence.

'Yes, truly.'

He sighed and reached out to stroke her hair away from her forehead. 'I couldn't bear to lose you,' he murmured, his voice deep with emotion. 'I know I can't expect you to feel the same way about me, but I love you, Karen. If there's anything . . .'

'But I do love you, Hal. I've loved you for a long, long time,' she said joyously.

'You . . . love me?' His voice was almost strangled with incredulity.

'Since soon after we were married,' she confessed gently.

'Oh God, no! No!' He bent his head down and rested it on hers. 'How can you forgive me all I've done?' he whispered hoarsely.

Karen lifted her arms and wrapped them around him. 'We're together, aren't we?' she soothed. 'Kiss me, Hal. Please?'

'Karen . . . Karen . . .' His mouth carried his deep yearning for her into a kiss that held a wealth of tenderness and wanting, and Karen responded with all the giving in her heart.

'I don't deserve you, my love,' he sighed, laying his cheek against hers. 'I should have known better than to marry you like that. I should have known that Kirsty would only speak the truth when she was dying. I was too damned bitter and twisted afterwards to work out what she meant, but she knew all right. She knew what you would mean to me.'

'Kirsty?' Karen did not understand what Hal was talking about. 'What did she say?'

He propped himself up to look down at her. His eyes glinted with intensity in the dim light. 'Don't you know?'

'How could I?'

'You described what she was feeling. I thought you two were telepathic.'

'Only about some things. Not anything we didn't want each other to know,' she explained.

He shook his head sadly. 'It was a terrible, terrible night, Karen. I can't even remember the explosion. When I came to, Kirsty was sobbing my name over and over. I opened my eyes and she was trying to staunch the blood from my chest-wound. I didn't know that she was bleeding to death as she spoke to me. She said I had to live, and she told me about David. Her words became slower, more slurred, and she slid on to the ground beside me. I struggled up, and only then did I see the huge gash in her thigh. People were running around. I called out for help, and someone came. Kirsty plucked at my arm . . .'

He lifted his hand and rubbed it across his eyes. 'She asked me to hold her, hold her tight. Then she said . . . "You met the wrong mirror, Hal, but I had to keep you. I loved you too much to let go. I gave her the baby, but I couldn't give you up. Promise me now . . . promise me you'll marry Karen." '

'The wrong mirror,' Karen echoed sadly. 'Poor Kirsty. How that must have hurt!'

'I could feel her slipping away from me, but her eyes kept pleading, so I promised. She smiled then, smiled as if her soul was at peace. And she died in my arms, that same smile lingering on her face. I can't remember being taken away from her. The next thing I knew I was being carried into a hospital.'

Hal hesitated, then continued with quiet deliberation. 'I think she had a death-wish that last year, Karen. Not consciously, but when I look back now . . . she knew that you were the woman I needed. There were times when the feeling I had for her was very akin to love—almost, but not quite. I think what she had kept from both you and me was tearing her apart. I'd never seen her look serene until I gave her my promise to marry you at the end.'

'And that's why you married me?'

'Part of it. Mostly I wanted David. If I got you I got David. I didn't feel I had to honour the promise to Kirsty after I found out about David, yet I couldn't forget I'd given it either. At the time the idea of making you marry me gave me a lot of satisfaction, like finally collecting the payment for a long-standing debt I was owed. Yet there was something compelling about you, Karen. At first I thought it was because you looked like Kirsty, but when I made love to you . . .'

'Yes,' Karen agreed dreamily, 'it confused me too. I thought I hated you, but I didn't.'

Hal's sigh was full of regret. 'I thought you couldn't possibly feel anything but hatred for me.'

'I tried to show you, Hal.'

'I just couldn't believe it. I'm sorry, love. I knew I was falling in love with you and I was going crazy, thinking of how badly and meanly I'd treated you. After that argument we had about Kirsty I just about gave up all hope of your ever loving me. Until Professor Bellamy prompted you into saying that you and Kirsty had been mirror-image twins. Then everything Kirsty had said fell into place, and I knew I couldn't give up, because she'd believed that I was right for you too. And that gave me hope.'

Karen gurgled with happy laughter. 'And I thought you had a lust for pregnant women!'

Hal leaned over and kissed her very lustfully. 'Only for this woman,' he concluded in a tone of rich satisfaction.

'Hal?'

'Mmmmh?' His mouth hovered teasingly over hers.

'Is it all right with you if we call our first-born

twin Kirsten?' she whispered hopefully.

'Whatever you want, my darling. If it's possible, I think that would keep Kirsty smiling, and I guess we owe her that. We might never have met at all.'

Karen sighed in relief. She had wanted that very much, and she was so glad that Hal had forgiven Kirsty for everything. 'And I thought Rowena would be nice for the second twin. Owen would like that.'

Hal chuckled with pleasure. 'My father will be the proudest grandfather alive!' He drew in a deep breath and kissed her some more. 'I love you, Karen. I love you so much I can hardly bear to be parted from you even for a little while, but I was supposed to ring for a nurse when you woke up.'

'It can wait. I love you too, Hal. I've been wanting to say it for so long, it needs a lot of saying.'

Some considerable time later a nurse popped her head into the room, and after a few theatrical coughs, proceeded to chide both of them for acting irregularly. Not standard procedure at all. But very satisfactory, Hal remarked, completely unabashed.

Dr Grayson was called, and Karen underwent another examination. A nurse brought her dinner, and Hal urged her to eat more than she had appetite for. She was given another injection to make her sleep comfortably. She made Hal promise to go home and get a proper rest and not to worry about her any more. Her last thought before she fell asleep again was about the roses whose scent had sweetened her awakening. They had been red roses—dark, velvety red. For love.

Karen felt brilliantly alive the next day. The pain of childbirth was completely forgotten. The twins were brought to her room, snuggled together in a special cot. Professor Bellamy accompanied them and happily expounded all his theories to Karen.

'They must be allowed to sleep together until such time as they choose to have separate beds. Now that they're named, always try to get their identities right. Confusion will distress them.'

Karen smiled and the Professor laughed. 'Well, you can't remember back to infancy, can you?'

'No. I was just remembering what Kirsty and I used to do when our parents called us by our wrong names.'

'Ah yes. Stubborn little mules, I recall your mother saying. And wouldn't wear name tags when you went to school. What was it you said? ... "We know who we are and it's up to everyone else to find out."'

Karen laughed as the Professor shook his head at her. 'You just wait, young lady! That's what's in store for you.'

He rambled on until the babies' feeding time, then supervised the handling of the twins. Kirsten had to be cradled in Karen's left arm, while a nurse cradled Rowena in her right arm. It was fascinating to watch them suck so knowingly. When they were once more tucked into their cot Professor Bellamy beamed approval and took his leave.

Hal arrived with Owen and David on his heels. David was jumping out of his skin with excitement, as fascinated by his baby sisters as everyone else was. Owen was glowing with pride. He gave Karen a warm hug and a kiss, declared she looked more beautiful than ever, said she had picked splendid names, and Hal was the luckiest man alive.

With which Hal agreed. He sat on the bed, holding her hand, his eyes so eloquently expressing his love that warm tingles ran around Karen's veins. She felt lucky too, as if she had just won the best and biggest lottery that life could ever offer. She had Hal and David and Kirsten and Rowena . . . a beautiful family circle of love. And Owen standing behind them in all his benevolence.

And Kirsty slid into Karen's mind . . . Kirsty giving her David, the baby Karen had longed for . . . Kirsty giving her Hal with her dying breath . . . Kirsty, knowing it all and suffering her private pain until at the end she could smile, having given away everything. And Karen closed her eyes and sent out a message with all her concentrated will-power . . .

If you can hear me, Kirsty, thank you. I understand it all now, and you'll always be with us, alive, loved, part of all of us. As one with me as you always were and always will be, my beloved sister. Thank you.

AUTHOR'S NOTE

Professor Bellamy would almost certainly have seen more than two cases of mirror-imaged identical twins in his life as a specialist; at the present moment there are at least three known cases in Australia. The incidence of this remarkable phenomenon is open to grave doubt, dependent upon who is taken as an authority on the subject. Figures vary as much as one birth in ten thousand, to one in millions. Possibly the discrepancy is due to a lack of recognition of such cases. To the author's knowledge there are at least two studies of international importance taking place on this phenomenon at the present time.

The only important deviation from fact in this story is that Karen's pregnancy was diagnosed as such a case from an ultra-sound scan. The mirror-image phenomenon is said to be undiagnosable before birth. However, the one set of mirror-imaged twins (who are boys) known to the author were diagnosed as such before they were born. Whom do you believe? All the author can say is that she is proud of the doctor who did the diagnosis, against all the odds, and was right.

Coming Next Month

Available in November wherever paperback books are sold, or through Harlequin Reader Service:

In the U.S.
901 Fuhrmann Blvd.
P.O. Box 1397
Buffalo, N.Y. 14240-1397

In Canada
P.O. Box 603
Fort Erie, Ontario
L2A 5X3

What the press says about Harlequin romance fiction...

"When it comes to romantic novels...
Harlequin is the indisputable king."
— *New York Times*

"...always with an upbeat, happy ending."
— *San Francisco Chronicle*

"Women have come to trust these
stories about contemporary people,
set in exciting foreign places."
— *Best Sellers*, New York

"The most popular reading matter of
American women today."
— *Detroit News*

"...a work of art."
— *Globe & Mail*, Toronto

ATTRACTIVE, SPACE SAVING BOOK RACK

Display your most prized novels on this handsome and sturdy book rack. The hand-rubbed walnut finish will blend into your library decor with quiet elegance, providing a practical organizer for your favorite hard-or soft-covered books.

Only $9.95

Approximately 16" x 8" when assembled

Assembles in seconds!

To order, rush your name, address and zip code, along with a check or money order for $10.70* ($9.95 plus 75¢ postage and handling) payable to *Harlequin Reader Service*:

Harlequin Reader Service
Book Rack Offer
901 Fuhrmann Blvd.
P.O. Box 1396
Buffalo, NY 14269-1396

Offer not available in Canada.

BKR-1A

*New York and Iowa residents add appropriate sales tax.

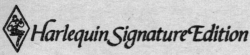

Penny Jordan

Stronger Than Yearning

He was the man of her dreams!

The same dark hair, the same mocking eyes; it was as if the Regency rake of the portrait, the seducer of Jenna's dream, had come to life. Jenna, believing the last of the Deverils dead, was determined to buy the great old Yorkshire Hall—to claim it for her daughter, Lucy, and put to rest some of the painful memories of Lucy's birth. She had no way of knowing that a direct descendant of the black sheep Deveril even existed—or that James Allingham and his own powerful yearnings would disrupt her plan entirely.

Penny Jordan's first Harlequin Signature Edition *Love's Choices* was an outstanding success. Penny Jordan has written more than 40 best-selling titles—more than 4 million copies sold.

Now, be sure to buy her latest bestseller, *Stronger Than Yearning*. Available wherever paperbacks are sold—in October.

Six exciting series for you every month... from Harlequin

Harlequin Romance·
The series that started it all

Tender, captivating and heartwarming...
love stories that sweep you off to faraway places
and delight you with the magic of love.

◆

Harlequin Presents·
Powerful contemporary love stories...as individual as the women who read them

The No. 1 romance series...
exciting love stories for you, the woman of today...
a rare blend of passion and dramatic realism.

◆

Harlequin Superromance®
It's more than romance... it's Harlequin Superromance

A sophisticated, contemporary romance-fiction
series, providing you with a longer,
more involving read...a richer mix of complex plots,
realism and adventure.

Harlequin American Romance™
Harlequin celebrates the American woman...

...by offering you romance stories written about American women, by American women for American women. This series offers you contemporary romances uniquely North American in flavor and appeal.

◆

Harlequin Temptation
Passionate stories for today's woman

An exciting series of sensual, mature stories of love...dilemmas, choices, resolutions... all contemporary issues dealt with in a true-to-life fashion by some of your favorite authors.

◆

Harlequin Intrigue
Because romance can be quite an adventure

Harlequin Intrigue, an innovative series that blends the romance you expect... with the unexpected. Each story has an added element of intrigue that provides a new twist to the Harlequin tradition of romance excellence.

Harlequin Books·

PROD-A-2

An enticing new historical romance!

Spring Will Come

SHERRY DeBORDE

It was 1852, and the steamy South was in its last hours of gentility. Camille Braxton Beaufort went searching for the one man she knew she could trust, and under his protection had her first lesson in love....

Available in October at your favorite retail outlet, or reserve your copy for September shipping by sending your name, address, zip or postal code, along with a check or money order for $4.70 (includes 75¢ postage and handling) payable to Worldwide Library to:

In the U.S.

Worldwide Library
901 Fuhrmann Blvd.
P.O. Box 1325
Buffalo, NY 14269-1325

In Canada

Worldwide Library
P.O. Box 609
Fort Erie, Ontario
L2A 5X3

Please specify book title with your order.

 WORLDWIDE LIBRARY

SPR-1